Jonas Watcher:
The Case of the Running Bag

Gene Poschman

DEDICATION

To Mary Lou,
My best Friend, My High School Sweetheart,
My Lover, My Wife,
My Life.

ACKNOWLEDGMENTS

I need to acknowledge, my wife, MaryLou, she is my primary reader and she can be brutally honest. My son, William, who is my second reader who looks for the hidden information, and is also brutally honest.

Although they have no idea that they played a part in my getting this book published, I would like to thank JA Konrath and Mark Coker, they have both provided me with invaluable information.

A special thanks to Doctor Don Knotts, who came late as a proof reader and did a remarkable job of showing me, my many misses. Needless to say hs is on the proofreading team for the next book, if he'll do it.

Table of Contents

On The Dock By The Bay

I was just waking up, I could hear chimes in the distance, twelve, midnight. I was cold and wet and coming down from the DT's. I looked up and I could see the underneath of the wharf above me. What the hell was I doing passed out on the docks? I had decided to quit drinking, cold turkey. The irony of the phrase leaped into my head. I needed a drink. I just couldn't get a drink. Now I remembered. I got kicked out of the bar because I had no money. I got arrested on a D and D and then twenty-four hours later I got tossed out of the drunk tank. I don't remember much after that. Now, I was lying down somewhere under the "Wharf", under a pier waking up to the undulating motion of a floating dock with the stench of sea water and decaying vegetation. I was not the least bit happy.

When I sat up I found I was at the water's edge and it was lapping up at the rotting wooden excuse for a dock I must have landed on. I know I had fallen because I was bruised and sore all over. I didn't seem to have any broken bones so I hadn't been in a fight. No one had tossed me down here, I had managed to stumble here all on my own. I moved to climb up the ladder on to the pier and get my bearings.

When I straightened up I discovered I was entangled in some kind of a net and I was cursing my luck, trying to shake it loose as I was climbing the ladder. Suddenly something from above hit me square in the chest and knocked me away from the ladder and the pier towards the water. I looked up as I was falling and I could see the shadow of whoever threw whatever hit me.

I yelled for help and I hit the water.

I was going down under the surface of the water. Whatever hit me was pretty heavy, and it and I were all tangled up in the net. That cursed net was either going to drown me or it was about to save my life. It was attached to the dock and it kept me and the dingus from being pulled down further into the water. I could see some light through the water and decided that way was up. I should have let go of the dingus, but I hung on to it, I don't know why.

I tried to focus on the light from the pier as I looked up through the water. The net had stopped pulling down, and though I was entangled, it was taut where it had been attached to the dock. I used it to pull myself back to the surface. When I broke through the water I took several deep breaths of air. The light from the pier waved through the mist, I heard a machine start up and a secondary light moved around above and then disappeared. I climbed out of the water onto the dock. The dingus, which I now realized was a large bag hung from the dock entangled in the net. I was soaked and I began to shiver from the cold.

I pulled the bag up onto the dock. I was

shaking so badly I couldn't open the latches on the bag. I had to sit down with my back against the ladder and try the latches again. Finally, I was able to open it up. There were a couple of weights in the bag. I pulled them out and tossed them into the water. I rummaged around in the bag examining the contents a little more. There were men's clothes, a suit, shoes, underwear, a train ticket, notebook, passport without a picture, some other odds and ends and an old Navy Colt forty-four. Shit!

I wondered why someone would throw the bag into the bay. Clearly to get rid of it. But why? The gun? I shook my head even more than it was shaking already. The inside of the bag was made of some kind of rubbery material, water tight, I checked the suit size, a tad big for me, but it was mostly dry and I wasn't. I started to strip off my clothes. It must have been a comical sight as I shivered while stripping. I used what I wasn't going to wear to dry off. Then I started putting clothes back on. I wasn't one for t-shirts, but I was cold. I finished dressing and suddenly realized how good it could feel to be dry again.

I climbed up the ladder with the bag and found a bench to sit on. I looked around, no one to be seen. I took a deep breath and explored the bag some more. There was something familiar about it. Not this particular bag, but I had seen others like it.

I found what I was looking for at the bottom

of the bag. If you weren't looking for it, you wouldn't have found it, a hidden pocket. This one was well hidden. I expected the pocket to come up empty. I was wrong. A business card with an address, keys and fifty double sawbucks, a grand. This bag sure didn't belong to whoever threw it over, nobody throws away a grand. It was a running bag. I had seen them before. In another life, I was an MP in the army. Men who were not quite straight would keep a hidden bag for a quick get away and that's what this was. Whoever it belonged to wasn't going to come looking for it. My guess was he had already made his final journey. I wonder if his body was floating somewhere else in the bay.

I took out the Colt, weighed it in my hand. I brought my arm back getting ready to hoist it into the bay and stopped. The gun was going to be bad news, probably used to kill somebody, tossing it into the bay was the smart thing to do. It was the one thing in the bag that would bring me trouble. I lowered my arm and looked at the gun again weighing it in my hand. What the hell, it might be leverage if I need it. I decided to keep it and I put it back into the bag.

I had a couple of bad years, and Fate was a Fickle Bitch, and at this moment she seemed to be smiling on me, so I decided to take the ride for a while. I searched through the bag a little more. There was a money belt in the hidden pocket and I put most of the money into it. I kept a couple of hundred for my immediate needs. I latched up the bag and got up to leave the pier. I was suddenly hungry and I went looking for the nearest all-night diner, I needed coffee and food, I wanted a scotch. Against character, I went for the food.

As I sat in the diner having coffee and something to eat I looked through the bag to see what else I could find out. The card with an address was a business card. It said Discrete Inquires Inc. It was the business card of a shamus, but why hidden? A phone number, an address, no name, discrete inquiries, indeed, I had the feeling that someone had got dead because of a discrete inquiry.

If I had any sense, I would lose the bag, keep the money, and live well at least for awhile. That is when it occurred to me. Maybe it was because I was finally warm, or had food in my stomach, or I just got over being dumped into the bay. I was close to the top of the ladder, in a sense I was at the most precarious position, whoever hit me with the bag, he had been waiting for me. He was not throwing away the bag. He was throwing my life away. Killing me. But who? Why?

The address was 891 Post, Suite 401, a couple of miles walk from the wharf, not too bad a part of town. Fate had not been good to me today, yesterday, it was past midnight, so now I have money in my pocket, a full stomach, and a curious nature; particularly when someone tries to kill me.

I decided to take a walk to the address on the

card. Maybe I would get some answers, I could always lose the bag later. I paid my tab, left a generous tip and left the diner. As I was walking towards Post I could have sworn I heard a woman laughing in the background.

The outside door to 891 Post was locked. One of the keys on the ring opened the door on to a lobby which was deserted. Curiouser and curiouser. It looked like it might be a small business building. There was an elevator across from a reception desk and down a short hall was a door that said stairs. I took the stairs. I figured it would be better if I didn't run into anyone this late. Fewer people would be using the stairs. I climbed to the fourth floor. The hallway was empty, the building was eerily quiet. Another key on the ring opened the door to suite 401 where Discrete Inquiries were made.

I entered the suite. Suite, there was a laugh. The room was small a couple of chairs for clients, a sofa, a desk for the receptionist, a coat tree, a locked file cabinet, a phone, an intercom and dust on the desk. I figured there might not have been a receptionist, at least for a week or so anyway. I shrugged, closed the door and made sure it was locked.

I let myself into the inner office. This was better, a nice sofa, power desk, client chairs, a really nice chair behind the desk, file cabinet, and a coat tree with an overcoat and a brown fedora. The desk was neat, clean blotter, a pen and pencil set that was monogrammed with an M and P, a phone and the other end of the intercom. There were a couple of doors off to one side. One turned out to be to a closet, and the other to a small bathroom with a sink and toilet. I suddenly had a yen for hot water on my face. I dropped the bag in the office and to my surprise there was hot water. Afterward, I wiped my face with a towel and looked around the office. The only light came in from the street through the window with Discrete Inquires written backwards.

Some of this didn't make sense. I don't think the running bag belonged to Mr. Discrete Inquiries, So why were his keys in it. I wondered if he knew who was not coming back or possibly who was interested in killing me. The outer office was almost spartan, but the inner office had comfort written all over it. This part of town was alright, but this office just didn't fit somehow.

Suddenly I was very tired, I really wanted a drink, but I knew that was the last thing I needed to do right now. I went back out to the outer office to the door and put a chair under the knob and jammed it home. I went back in to the inner office and took the colt out of the bag. I checked to see if it was loaded, it had five cartridges in the cylinder.

I hadn't really done anything wrong, but I was an uninvited guest and the colt should provide sufficient persuasion for anyone taking exception to my presence. At least it should give me time to tell my side of things. I remember yawning and lying down on the sofa, I wondered what time it was.

Discrete Inquiries

My dreams were fragmented with my time as an MP in Europe. A number of faces passed before me as I interviewed them. The shadow above me at the pier kept popping up, but no face appeared with it. I dreamt of my argument with my superior's in the MP's. They kept pounding on the table to drive a point home. Something was banging in my head. No not in my head, the door. I really like waking from an unrestful sleep slowly. I like to stretch, yawn, and stretch again. But the banging startled me I jerked awake and fell on the floor.

"Shit!"

"Mickey, Mickey are you in there? The door is locked! Open Up!"

"Yeah, Yeah, just a minute," I said.

My mind was ablaze of reasons I am here, and none of them made sense, even to me in my waking stupor. I decided to see who it was and play it by ear. I yelled I was coming, I stuffed the colt into the bag, and latched it up. I was still wiping the sleep from my eyes as I pulled the chair from the door and slowly opened it with my foot as a door stop.

"You're not Mickey," said a heavyset man in a trench coat and a matching rumpled fedora that screamed underpaid cop.

"Uh, no I'm Not," I said, letting him set the

pace.

"You his new partner?" he asked.

I wasn't quite sure how to answer, because I wasn't, and he might know that, so I temporized.

"I'm not sure," I said.

"Good answer, I wouldn't be sure of anything Mickey Philips does either. Say can I come in?"

"I don't mean to be rude, but who are you?" I asked.

Reverse the roles, put the other man on the defensive, and see what I can learn.

"Oh, sure," he opened his coat and showed me his badge. "Lieutenant Sanders, SFPD."

I stepped back and opened the door and let the Lieutenant in.

"Sorry, Lieutenant, uh Mickey didn't tell me someone would be calling today. Gave me keys so I could flop here last night." I shrugged.

"By the way what's your name?" he asked.

I had thought about handing him a phony moniker, but that Fickle Bitch was watching me and I was pretty sure that, in this case, honesty would be the best policy, otherwise I might end up in the clink. Besides I hadn't really done anything wrong, I kept telling myself that, except flop for the night. I could tell the flatfoot was already suspicious of me.

"Watcher, Jonas Watcher," I said holding out my hand. He took it in a firm handshake without any contest. I responded in kind. I had a strange feeling I could like the Lieutenant, he didn't actually smile, but the tension was less. I wasn't out of the woods though, but I wasn't about to be hauled off to jail, not just yet.

"You ain't seen Mickey, today." More statement than question.

"I got tossed the keys and the address last night, and to be honest, I can't say Mickey was the one who gave them to me." I couldn't be more truthful than that, right.

We went into the inner office and I took the sofa while the Lieutenant circled the desk and then sat down in one of the client chairs. In his little walk about the desk, he looked around. He had determined, I hadn't rummaged through the desk and everything else in the office was as it should be. I was glad I hadn't succumbed to that particular urge last night.

The Lieutenant reached into his coat pocket and pulled some papers. He handed them out to me and I took them, I tried not to act surprised.

"That's the application for your PI License under Mickey, his info is already filled out, you fill out yours and drop them by the precinct later today, and I'll see they get processed".

So Mickey was looking to add someone to his... staff.

"We have to do a background check," he continued, "but if nothing flags, you'll have your license in a couple of weeks. I told Mickey you could work under his... as temporary help until yours comes through."

"Thanks, Lieutenant, I 'm uh..."

"When he asked me for the papers, he was still deciding on candidates, that's why your part is blank. You got a piece? Registered?"

"There's an old Navy Colt in the bag there, but it's not registered to be carried as concealed"

The Lieutenant leaped to his feet, startling me, "Are you kidding me? I thought Mickey was kidding me. Can I see it?"

I knew that colt was going to be trouble. I was hesitant, but I had gone this far, in for a dime, might as well go for the whole buck. But I didn't want him going through the bag, might be something in there that would hang me up.

"Could you toss me the bag?" I asked.

The Lieutenant bent down and picked it up by the handle, it was still wet. He watched me closely as he handed it over.

"Dropped it in a puddle," I said. I slowly opened the bag enough for the colt to be visible, then I held it up so the Lieutenant could see it.

"Go ahead take it out," I said. If he was concerned about fingerprints, he might not take it.

He reached in slowly and lifted it out admiringly, he weighed it in his hand and turned it so he could examine it more closely. So help me if that gun is a murder weapon...

"Single action, hmm. Loaded?" he asked.

I looked at him and he suddenly grinned,

"Stupid question." He clicked out the cartridges from the cylinder and handed them to me. Then he spun the gun around a couple of times, cocked back the hammer, aimed at the window, and pulled the trigger. Click! Okay, so fingerprints weren't an issue.

"That'll drop a man. Can't really carry it concealed, the bulge would stick out, but a nice piece" He spun it around and handed it to me butt first. I took it and dropped it into the bag along with the cartridges.

"Paperwork to carry, it is there too. Fill it out and get it in before you go to work, okay?"

The Lieutenant turned to leave and I walked with him to the outer door. We shook hands and he was gone. I closed and locked the door. That was just too lucky, he was expecting someone here, either Mickey Philips or his new partner?

I went back into the inner office and dropped on the sofa shaking my head. I needed to get out of here and fast. Maybe the running bag belonged to whoever Mickey was going to hire. But then why was it used as a club to take me out? Since the bag had been lost, or was going to be lost in the bay with my body, Mickey's unnamed partner was dead or held captive somewhere about to be dead. Sooner or later one or the other was going to turn up and I didn't want to be around when crap started falling out of the sky.

Suddenly I was hungry again, and I wanted a drink. I had a little time before things got too strange. I figured I'd go down to the diner on the corner, grab some grub, come back, pick up the bag and leave town. I would hold off having a drink until I was in the clear. I removed the money belt and dropped it in the bag, no need to tempt the Fickle Bitch. I put the bag under the desk hidden behind the modesty panel and headed out. I really wanted a drink, but eating was a better idea, and a newspaper. I had to see if anything had been reported that might help me figure out where I stood.

At the diner, I took a stool at the counter that gave me a view of who was coming in and signaled to the waitress for service. She was a cute kid, early twenties, blonde and fairly new to waiting tables. She still had a freshness about her and a spring in her step that indicated she was new or an eternal optimist.

"What'll ya have?" she asked.

"The number one on your menu, coffee, and a newspaper, if you got one."

"Sure, but we're out of newspapers, unless you don't mind a used one."

"Sold," I said, "I'll take it."

Several people came and went, but nothing exciting happened. I was beginning to feel like I was overreacting. The waitress brought me a rumpled paper that seemed intact, and she was quick with the coffee and the breakfast. I leafed through the paper and didn't find anything that would help clear up what happened to Mickey's partner. I even waded through the classifieds, in case there was something there. Since I came up empty, I decided to grab the bag and blow this town. I had money. L. A. was looking pretty good to me just now. I headed back to pick up the bag and then I was outta here.

I arrived back in the office building, and this time I took the elevator up. I stepped out... Did I say, Fate was a Fickle Bitch? When I got back to the office she had made other arrangements for me, in the form of a gorilla dressed as a chauffeur carrying a briefcase and a lady, and I mean one with class. She was a tall brunette, older, but she would still leave men drooling in her wake as she walked passed. They were standing in front of the office door, waiting. I could ignore them and walk on by, but the bag under the desk had the money belt, and I wasn't about to leave without it. I walked up to the mismatched pair and introduced myself, using my real name and associating myself with Mickey Philips. The woman was calm, cool and collected, the body building chauffeur looked like a deer caught in the headlights.

"You're not William Mason," she said.

"No, like I said, I'm Jonas Watcher, I'm kind of holding the fort until Mickey gets back. Do you want to leave a message?" I asked, hoping she would decide to come back later.

"We had better come in," she said. "I have something to leave and I want to make sure it's safe in Mr. Philips office."

I nodded, smiled and I unlocked the door. She watched me closely as I opened the door. Having keys, and knowing which one to use on the door seemed to ease the lady's mind. I escorted her into the inner office and the chauffeur followed us in. I had the feeling driving was only a small part of his duties, muscle and security were probably the other two. I indicated for them to sit down in the client chairs while I took up sitting in the chair behind the power desk. I pulled open a drawer and took out a pad and pencil and set to take notes like it was second nature.

"Sorry, no secretary..." I said.

"Yes, I know, getting married, Mr. Philips already told me. My name is Elizabeth Stanton, from New York, are you familiar with my case?"

You could have knocked me over with a feather, she was a lady, a really rich lady, and as for the case, there were several possibilities, her father-in-law was rumored connected to the New York underworld, her husband had disappeared, there have been threats against her, she was a queen in New York Society, her brother was running for senator in Massachusetts, and she was hosting some big art show in San Francisco, and she had been seen in the company of some Hollywood Producer in Los Angeles.

"I'm just taking care of the office right now, Mrs Stanton. Mickey has a secure box here in the desk and I can open it for you to store whatever it is you have for him."

She turned her head to the chauffeur, "Joseph, take out the file."

The chauffeur opened the briefcase and rummaged a bit looking for the "file". As he shifted a bulge under his arm became more than noticeable. Ape-man was packing. I decided to continue to play it straight, even though as I kept doing so, I seemed to be getting deeper into something I knew nothing about and it was getting more difficult to extricate myself. He pulled out a folder, put it on the desk, and slid it over to me. I picked it up and started to put it away in the secure drawer when Mrs Stanton stopped me.

"No, no, I want you to read it, study it. Mr. Philips was quite adamant that whoever we met here would be the operative to handle my case."

Jeez, everyone was expecting to meet someone here, and I seemed to be the only person present, and I wasn't suppose to be here. The Fickle Bitch and her sisters were out there somewhere laughing up a storm at the predicament I just found myself in. I slowly opened the folder and briefly leafed through the papers.

"I don't expect you to read it now, Mr. Watcher, but I believe the retainer there should be enough to get you started looking in to where my husband is. The last few checks I sent him were picked up here in San Francisco at general delivery. I must go down to Los Angeles for a day, and I when I get back you can update me. I'll be staying at The Palace."

Of course she would. The retainer was a cashiers check made out to cash for two grand. I nodded knowingly, not looking the least surprised, and rose as Mrs Stanton stood up. "Joseph, we are going, Mr. Watcher has much to do. We'll see ourselves out."

I watched as they left, the Chauffeur seemed confused and somewhat distressed. She on the other hand was cool and swayed that maybe left me drooling just a little bit.

This was getting too crazy. I woke up a little over twelve hours ago hurting, hungover and broke absolutely nothing going on in my life. Now, someone has attempted to kill me, I was sitting on a years plus income and mixed up in something that could only blow up in my face and I was seriously considering not running for the hills. I couldn't go to Los Angeles, she would be there. I know it's a big place but Fate was messing with me. I didn't dare take the two G's without looking into her husband's whereabouts.

Any minute now, Mickey Philips would come through that door and all hell would break loose. Then all of a sudden it hit me! I could be walking into something where I was going to be the biggest patsy of all time. Two people are looking for someone and here I am. I'm him, except I'm not him. And that him could be dead and who killed him... the only viable suspect, me!

I had been playing it fast and loose and so far I was still on my feet, and I intended to stay that way. If I boogied now, it would all come down on me. I had to do two things, find out where Mrs Stanton's husband is, and locate William Mason, and if he's dead prove I didn't make him that way. And where the hell was Mickey Philips.

I sat down at the desk and started filling out the forms. Luckily no one came in while I was giving the police a breakdown on my life up until now. When I finished, I put the folder that Mrs Stanton had brought including the check into the secure drawer and headed for the local precinct. I hoped the Lieutenant would still be happy to see me, because right now I figured the roof was about to cave in on me.

I took a deep breath, my next step, apply for a PI license and carry permit, and stay sober. It was the only way I was going to get out of this alive. And you can stop laughing you stupid Fickle Bitch.

An Uninvited Guest

I turned the corner and started towards the precinct. A paper boy was hawking the latest afternoon edition. Dock strike, bad unemployment, and SF Private Investigator found dead in Sacramento. My blood ran cold. I had a feeling I was about to walk straight into the gates of hell. I half expected the motto above the police station door to read "...Abandon all hope ye who enter here." Running was not an option, the best I could hope for is that either the Lieutenant wasn't here, or I had an iron clad alibi.

Two things struck me when I entered the precinct, every desk sergeant in the country looks the same, and when you don't want to find a cop, you will. I identified myself to the desk sergeant, who was expecting me and he picked up the phone and got Lieutenant Sanders for me. Moments later the Lieutenant arrived.

"Hello, Lieutenant, I brought the papers."

"I'm glad you did, why don't you come into my office and we'll have a little talk," he said.

The good news was he didn't say I was under arrest, the bad news... I was still waiting for that one.

We really did go the Lieutenant's office, I had half expected him to haul into a small room with a single light and a big goon who would do the persuading for me to answer questions the way they wanted me to.

"Sit down, Watcher, we need to talk." he said.

I sat, so did he. I held out the forms.

"You still want these?" I asked.

"As a matter of fact, I do."

He briefly read through them, his face took on an air of surprise.

"This is pretty thorough, we don't usually get this much information. You really were an MP in the army?"

I nodded.

"If this checks out... You still want the license?"

"More than you can know," I replied. "I take it the kid hawking papers outside was talking about Mickey Philips."

"He was."

"Any idea what happened, the kid yelled murdered. Any idea who did it?"

The Lieutenant pushed back his chair and eyed me slowly, he was sizing me up, I just wasn't sure if it was for a noose or not.

"Not my case, it happened in Sacramento, and they made it clear, they didn't want me butting in."

"Lieutenant, give me something here. I have had a pretty crazy twelve hours and I got a feeling it's going to get stranger before it straightens out."

"I know two things," he said, "He was killed with a thirty-eight, and you didn't kill him, at least not directly."

"And how do you know the second part?"

"You got an iron-clad alibi, when Mickey Philips was being shot down, I was banging on his office door, and you answered it."

"It hit the papers that fast?" I asked.

"It's an extra, the morning edition with a new headline."

Now it was my turn to push back in my chair. The Lieutenant knew I didn't do it, and I'm pretty sure he knows I didn't have it done, no motive, so just what did the Lieutenant want.

"So Lieutenant, what's in the wind that you are not telling me?"

"William Mason," he said.

"Oops," I replied

"You knew about him?" he asked.

"Someone thought I might be him."

I cocked my head to one side and stared at the Lieutenant for a moment or two. I don't know whether Mrs Stanton was playing me or not, but the Lieutenant had been, to some degree. I needed information, and he wanted something, it was time for us to deal. I indicated he start.

"Mickey never said anything about a Navy Colt forty-four," he said. "I lied. The paperwork was for William Mason, but his information wasn't included because I didn't have any, and I sure as hell wasn't going to fill in any blanks for him, not knowing who he was.

"I decided to make like the forms were for an

unknown. Since they weren't filled out it was easy to do. Didn't know who you were, but you had Mickey's keys and you didn't appear to be hiding anything obvious. But when you mentioned the gun, I decided to throw you off a bit. I was pretty sure you weren't carrying it, and as I said that baby packs a big punch, so I wanted to know where it was. Also, I need to know more about you. Mickey didn't hand keys to just anyone, so that was in your favor. Your answers were just straight and vague enough that I had no cause to run you in, but something wasn't right, so I figured I'd see what you were up to."

"I don't know who actually gave me the keys," I said, "they came as part of a package that deposited me into the bay."

He looked at me oddly. I wasn't going to give him the whole story, just enough to be straight with him. I explained about finding the keys, the gun, and the clothes in the bag. I didn't tell him about it being a running bag, or the passport or the money. I didn't want him to get self-righteous on me and tell me to return it. I wrapped up telling him I flopped at the office.

"I got some food and checked out the address. It was clean and dry, and I needed a place to stay. I hoped I could talk myself out of any trouble if someone showed up."

The Lieutenant started chuckling and shook his head.

"That's the damnedest story I have heard all

year. It's got to be true." He held up the forms I filled out. "If this is straight, and you would be stupid to give me something that wasn't, you can still have the license, if you want it."

But we weren't done. The Fickle Bitch hadn't put in her two cents worth and I was waiting for her surprise. The Lieutenant didn't take long in delivering it.

"I don't like being frozen out of a case that I know is going to come back to San Francisco, even though it started in the state capitol. That's what's happening here. Mickey Philips wasn't a best buddy, but he was a straight shamus, and we helped each other out now and again. Until something brings his murder into my jurisdiction I can't do dick. I got superiors to report to. You, on the other hand, are a private tek, and you have free reign. I can provide you information, you can do the leg work. Bring this case back to San Francisco so I can get on board officially."

"What about William Mason? Why not contact him?" I asked.

"He is in the wind, as far as I know, he's a ghost. Besides he hasn't filed any forms to be a PI, and you have. If he shows up, I'll deal with him then. He may even be a part of all this."

We talked a bit more, and I now had a firmer handle on... Who am I kidding, this was still an illusion, but I wasn't alone. Philips being dead only bought me an ally for as long as it didn't look like I had him killed. I had to get back to the office and dig through Philips files. Lieutenant Sanders had me wait for a bit while he got me a temporary PI license, the real one would show up in the Discrete Inquiries office in a couple of weeks. When he came back he had a temporary gun permit too.

"You'll have to bring the gun in for the boys to run a ballistics on it. Relax, there isn't anything outstanding on a Navy Colt forty-four, so you should be in the clear for now," he said

We had an understanding. He would meet me later in the office and go over what I had learned after I'd done a little sleuthing. That was a laugh, but the best place for me to go was back to the office and dig into Mickey Philips files. I decided to begin with Mrs Stanton's case, after all, that one had a two grand paycheck tied to it.

I grabbed a sandwich and a coke from the diner and headed up in the elevator to the fourth floor. The doors opened and it seemed too quiet to me. I stepped out slowly and a man was coming from the direction of the office. Collar pulled up, hat pulled down, he didn't want to be recognized. As we passed and he stepped into the elevator the waft of cologne that hit me was overwhelming. I might not be able to identify him in a lineup, but I would be able to smell him coming from two blocks away. I walked passed the office like I was going somewhere else until the elevator closed, then I made a dash to the door of the office. Someone had tried to jimmy the lock. There were a couple of doors between me and the colt and I wanted that gun loaded and in my hand in case my nose started screaming again.

I didn't fumble keys and I slid through the door, planted my sandwich and coke on the receptionists desk, grabbed a chair and jammed it into the door very quickly. Then I set the lock. I was at the desk in the inner office, bag opened, gun out and loaded and then I just sat there for a couple of seconds, remembering to breathe. I don't know which I noticed first, the sound at the door or the pungent smell of my visitor. I stood up and decided to see what he wanted, but the breaking glass, and the fumbling of the door and chair gave me cause to wait before I offered an invitation.

"Miserable shamus trick," I heard him say.

Then he busted through the door, he raised up a snub-nosed thirty-eight in my direction, it was the last thing he did!

When adrenalin hits everything goes in slow motion, I already had the colt positioned, I cocked the hammer and pulled the trigger twice. I didn't really see the bullets leave the barrel and travel the twelve feet to their destination, but I did see as each one hit its target. Although he had busted the door in, he hadn't really gotten through it, his single shot went down and wide as he was knocked back by the impact of the forty-four slugs.

I suppose I heard each projectile as it thumped into his chest, I saw what seemed like dust jump from his coat. The look of surprise on his face told me he didn't expect me, or whoever was here to be armed. By the time he hit the wall on the other side of the hall he was dead. He slowly collapsed sliding against the wall leaving a blood trail down to the floor.

I walked to the door and slowly looked around. Nobody came out into the hall to see what happened. Curiosity killed the cat. I guess they figured they'd find out what was going on when the police arrived. I backed into the office towards the receptionists desk, just in case there was more than one visitor waiting to see me. I picked the receiver up and dialed the precinct.

"Lieutenant Sanders, please..."

I had put the gun down on the inner office desk and waited there. I kept an eye on the inner office door and the door to the hallway. Somewhere in the background I swear I could hear some women laughing.

Paranoia Doesn't Mean You're Wrong

The Lieutenant entered with another plain clothed detective and several uniforms. Sanders looked at the body from different angles while the other detective walked over by me. The Lieutenant had a couple of uniforms start knocking on doors while he had others block off the body. Then he came over to me and told the other detective to pick up my gun with a handkerchief.

"Jeez, Watcher," said Lieutenant Sanders, "I know I told you to keep your gun handy, but I didn't expect you to shoot someone before we got together this evening."

"It wasn't my idea, I was perfectly willing to talk to the man, but clearly he had other ideas. He tried to break in earlier, so I suspect, there is something in here he wanted to get his hands on real bad."

"How do you know it was him? Maybe someone else."

"Did you smell him? I passed him by the elevator, got more of a whiff than I wanted. When I got to the door, the odor was really strong and there were jimmy marks on the door jam. I wasn't sure if he was going to come back or not, so I got the colt, and loaded it. I heard someone at the door I started out to see who it was, and he broke in and was raising his piece and I chose not to be the one to end up dead."

"How you know he's giving you the right scoop, Lieutenant, maybe he shot first." said the detective with Lieutenant Sanders.

"I did, I wasn't waiting to see why he was raising his weapon. He was breaking in, and I was in his way," I replied.

"Sergeant Simon Church, this is Jonas Watcher, now go over and take a look at the body," said Lieutenant Sanders.

Simon obeyed and stopped short. "Crap, that's Perfume Eddy, we got a warrant on him. He's a small-time crooked son of a bitch. We suspected he was a button man, but what's he doing in this part of town? This ain't his usual haunt."

"Still think, Watcher's not giving it to us straight?" asked the Lieutenant.

"Maybe they was in it together." Simon wasn't going to let it go.

"In what together, Simon, try not to think, just go down to the lobby and see to it the coroner gets up here to the right place, I don't want someone having a heart attack, if he knocks on the wrong door." Then he turned to me, "It almost happened once, someone answered the door and he said he was the coroner and where was the dead body. The poor sap almost provided him with one.

"Let's you and me go back into the office, I know you haven't done any sleuthing, it's been a little more than an hour since we last talked, but maybe we can figure out why this mug was here."

"Actually I have a file that may be part of

this, something that turned up before I was at the precinct."

I opened up the secure drawer and retrieved Mrs Stanton's file sans the check then we settled down into the client chairs to go through it. The Lieutenant didn't need to know everything. I tossed the file onto the desk and we sifted through the papers.

It was a report from National Investigators Inc, a high-end detective agency, they had operatives, not teks. They were big back East, and were moving to the west coast, their aim was to take on the Pinkertons to be the big gorilla in the industry. It was a detailed report on Martin Stanton, Mrs Stanton's husband.

The Stanton's were well to do, but the Parks, Mrs Stanton's maiden name, were in the area of super wealthy. When Martin Stanton refused to become an attorney and join his father's firm, he was disinherited. The recently married couple didn't care, Mrs Stanton had inherited money from her grandmother and an aunt, and that didn't include the possible money from her living father, who doted on his children.

Stanton wanted to be a painter, and he actually had some talent, but he was studying more and painting less. Apparently he was really interested in his models. One day he up and disappeared. A couple of months later, National found Martin in Miami, Florida and they let Mrs Stanton know where he was. She didn't ask for a divorce, in fact she went to Miami and met with Martin. They spent some time together, and she went back to New York. She sent him a monthly allowance and continued to visit him from time to time. That went on for a while, and he vanished again.

National was back on the case, and they found out he was in New Orleans, but they never actually contacted him. He was there several months before he skipped again. It took National another couple of months to find him, this time in Los Angeles.

Elizabeth Stanton has got to be the most persistent woman there is or maybe she's just gullible. She sent him money in Los Angeles, but in fact she hadn't seen him since Miami. When he moved to San Francisco, he let her know where he was going but there was no forwarding address. He told her she could get in touch with him in care of general delivery at the main post office.

"Now she's in San Francisco to what?" I stared at the Lieutenant. Suddenly his eyes got really big.

"We'll need to contact National," he said.

"How come?" I asked.

"Look at the bottom of the last three reports," he said.

They were signed off by a senior operative of National, named Sam Parrish.

Was there a faint echo of a woman's laughter in the air?

While the Lieutenant and I were going through the National file, the body had been examined and taken away. Some people had come in and done some cleanup. The police barricade had been taken down and as evening was falling, everything was pretty much back to normal. The building Super had some workmen replacing the door. Simple Simon and the Coroner were still hanging around to talk to the Lieutenant. Simon went first.

"The uniforms and I talked with the other tenants, and other than concern to get back to business, we didn't get much. One secretary down the hall had seen the guy trying to break in and then she ducked away before any of the shots had been fired. She did put a call into the police, and we have a record of that. It looks like the shamus' version of events is fairly accurate."

That must have been hard for him to admit, I thought.

The Coroner started to give Lieutenant Sanders the details, but Sanders kept interrupting him.

"The cause of death was," the Coroner started to say.

"Yeah, two forty-four slugs to the heart," said the Lieutenant.

The Coroner sighed. "He had been drinking, did you know that!"

"No, I couldn't smell anything over the perfume."

"I guess I got closer to his mouth than you did," said the Coroner.

"That's not something I would let get around, Doc.," said the Lieutenant.

The Coroner harrumphed. "He had been in a fight recently. I suspect he won, you might want to look for the loser."

The Lieutenant looked at me, "You didn't have an altercation with the gentleman before the gun fight, did you?"

"No, I wouldn't have stayed within his vicinity long enough, and if we had been in a fist fight, he would not have come out the winner. But he would still be alive." I held up my hands, there was no bruising on my knuckles to indicate I had been in a fight.

"Thought Not. Doc, whoever fought with him, didn't kill him."

"How do you know that?" asked the Coroner.

"Because, I'm the one who shot him," I said.

"Then what am I doing here?" asked the Coroner.

"Dead man shot, Doc, you gotta be called." said the Lieutenant.

"Then, it's a closed case," said the Coroner.

"Not likely," said the Lieutenant. "It is part of a bigger case, so when you get back to your lab, process him really good, I want to know where the bastard's has been for the last couple of days."

"Okay," said the Coroner, and he left.

"Simon, you look into his associates, he wanted in here bad. He was willing to kill for whatever he was looking for. Get some guys from the lab in here, I want every report read and notated, I want to know what Mickey Philips was working on."

Okay, Lieu, I'm on it." said Simon as he started to leave.

The Lieutenant stopped him. "Simon give me the Colt."

"Uh, Lieu,..." Simon started to object.

"I'll see it gets to ballistics in the morning."

Simon took the Colt from his belt and gave it to Lieutenant Sanders. Then he eyed me with a look of distrust. Then he left.

"I don't think he likes me very much," I said.

"He doesn't, because you're smart, but don't underestimate him,"

"By the way, I thought you couldn't look into Mickey Philip's murder," I said.

"I can't, but I got a killing here, and it might be related, and that gives me an in," he said. "It looks like you don't have to go to Sacramento just yet. Ironically, your little shooting here is just what I need to keep my superiors happy, at least for about forty-eight hours anyway. I still can't go digging into who killed Mickey in Sacramento, but I can look into what Mickey Philip's was working on that brought Eddie here. I can gather background as to why this mug was breaking into the office, and why he might want to kill a partner of Mickey Philips. Like I said, it's an in, so I don't have to sit on my hands, waiting.

"Look," he continued, "you take Mrs Stanton's file here and find out about..."

"William Mason," I finished for him. "That works for me. Look can I get my stuff out of here, I would just as soon as grab a room somewhere else. I'll let you know where as soon as I flop. I would rather not have any notoriety about what happened here, especially if I'm going to be of any use to you. Additionally I don't want to scare Mrs Stanton away. After all, she's my first client and maybe our best lead as to what happened to Mickey Philips."

"Yeah, that's okay, just keep me up to date."

He handed me back my colt, "You may want to keep this just in case someone else is around. But try using it as a threat rather than blowing someone else away, okay. And make sure Ballistics gets that in the morning, or I'll come looking for you. You got about 15 minutes before the boys show up, so get your stuff and take off, I'll see they lock up."

I went back to the desk and dropped the colt into the bag, I pulled some stuff from the secure drawer in Mickey's desk and took Mrs Stanton's folder. I turned back to the Lieutenant, "National will be closed back East, they got an office here in the city?"

"Yeah, it's small, but I'll get you the information on it, maybe they can get you a lead on William Mason."

I smiled and nodded. There was a residential hotel a couple of blocks away, I decided to go there, it was close to the office and the precinct, and right now that was just what I needed. I wanted a drink, but that was not going to happen, it would be that kind of stupid move that would probably cost me my life.

After Enlightenment, You Keep Working

The Marlon's Garden Apartments was a step
up in residential hotels, in that the rooms were
studios with private baths. I had been watching my
back the entire way from the office. I'm sure I
looked a little like a nut case. When I walked into
the lobby and asked for a room, I could feel some
hesitancy, but when I ponied up a months rent in
advance, the receptionist turned decidedly
warmer. She had a room on the second floor away
from the street and the elevator, but it still had a
view of the lobby, that suited me fine. I signed in
under my real name and declined the special
services that the receptionist eagerly suggested
would be available.

I went up to my room and checked it out. An
alcove on the right when I first came in substituted
for a kitchen, there was an ice box, sink and a hot
plate on the counter. The room was adequate size,
maybe sixteen by twenty feet. There was a
Murphy bed on the long wall with inexpensive
armoires on either side. A door at the end to a
bathroom, and a window that overlooked the
garden area. It had shades and a curtain and that
suited me too. A small table for eating, and a
couple of reasonable chairs for sitting. Added to
this they had a phone. I had noticed the PBX next
to the reception area, so I wouldn't need to go out
to make some phone calls. This would do until I

could figure out where I really wanted to live.

I examined the armoires closely and decided I could create a false bottom under one of them that would survive fairly close scrutiny, I would stop at a nearby hardware store for the tools I would need. The table was large enough to serve as a simple desk. I would still use the office during the day. I needed a receptionist, the diner below the office had a job board. I would check that out, maybe the folks there could recommend someone. Local diners had a good rep for knowing their clientele, and they might be able to help me find someone reliable.

Since it was time to eat, I headed for the diner, I could get some food, check out the job board, get some local gossip and set myself up as an upstanding citizen. I debated about carrying the colt, and decided against it. There was a slight indentation in back one of the armoires, so I concealed it there for the time being. I hung up and put into drawers what few clothes I had. I was going to have to do some shopping in the morning, but for the rest of the night I was going to just be a guy having dinner after a particularly hard day at the office.

When I arrived at the diner, the morning waitress was getting ready to leave. She was joined by an older woman from the kitchen. I asked if they might give me some advice about the job board and who would be a good for a new receptionist.

"Hey, I'll foot the bill for a meal here, if you wouldn't mind?" I said.

They looked at each other as if they were party to some kind of a joke that I knew nothing about.

"Mom, Dad is working late tonight," the younger woman said. "It would be nice not to have to cook, and let someone else take care of the dishes for a change." Mother and daughter, that must have been the joke. I hoped the mother didn't see this as a come on, the young woman was cute, as I said before, but she was about fifteen years too young for me.

"I'm straight about this," I said, "I am working upstairs for a PI, and the receptionist is gone, and I need someone to fill in for a while. It's mostly answering the phone, taking messages, and maybe a little light typing. You can check with the local precinct."

"We'll take you up on the dinner offer, Mr..." said the mother.

"Watcher, Jonas Watcher. Let's grab a booth and talk." I said.

They picked a booth about midway back, it was well-lit and away from the front and kitchen doors. I made a mental note, it was also fairly quiet.

A waitress came over, and handed us menus. "Betty, you eating here, tonight with the kid? Who's the gent?"

"Al is always bragging what a good cook he

is, I figure I'd see for myself," she replied. "This is Mr. Watcher, he works upstairs..."

"Oh yeah, the new shamus with Mickey Philips. A shame about Mickey, and the shooting up there. Were you involved, Mr. Watcher?"

"Maggie, really!"

"It's okay," I said, "Mrs..."

"Just call me, Betty, everyone does. And Shanna is my daughter."

"Yeah, Maggie," I said. " I was involved, I just don't like to advertize it, that's all. Lieutenant Sanders cleared me of any wrong doing. The Guy was a trigger happy burglar, that's all."

"Say, Maggie, how about tonight's special, and I'll have coffee," said Betty.

"Me too, and coffee," said Shanna.

"Make it three all around," I said.

Maggie took the order to the window behind the counter and the three of us returned to our conversation.

"I took a look at the job board by the door, and I saw some notes from women looking for work. I figured you might know who would best fit the bill for the office upstairs. It would start out temporary, but it could become full time. To be honest, I'm not sure how to pick a receptionist."

Maggie came back with coffees and hung for a bit until Betty indicated a couple coming through the door, and Maggie was off to serve them.

"Why don't you apply, Mom?" said Shanna.

"Look, Shanna, I'm sure Mr. Watcher, is looking for someone a little younger."

Shanna turned to me, "Mom's, cooking here is temp. She worked as a secretary for the police department, for about five years before I came along, and she has done some temp work for them. She knows everyone, and she would love to get out of this diner."

"She means, she would love for me to be out of this diner," said Betty.

"Lieutenant Sanders knows her," said Shanna with a bit of a knowing look. "He would vouch for her."

I looked at the two of them for a few moments. I didn't hear any laughing in the distance from the Fickle Bitch.

"I'll be honest, Betty, you are exactly what I am looking for, I don't want any kid, and the clientele may need a firm hand. If you're interested, check with me in the morning when I come in for breakfast."

"What's it pay?" asked Shanna.

"Shanna, really!" said Betty.

"Fifty bucks a week," I said.

"Are you, serious?" asked Shanna, to her mother, "Mom, you gotta say yes".

"I'll think about it. We'll talk again in the morning, okay, Mr. Watcher?"

"Fair enough," I replied, "Besides, our dinner is arriving."

Maggie again took her time about serving, hoping to catch some conversation, but it was all small talk and she soon lost interest. Al was a good cook, at least as far as I was concerned. Shanna indicated her mother was better, but Betty acknowledged that Al wasn't just bragging, Meat, potatoes, vegetables, rolls and apple pie for dessert made a pretty good meal.

The two women made good company, it was like being a regular Joe, and it felt nice. We parted company just outside the door, I headed for my hotel and they headed for the bus. I remember thinking that Betty would make a good receptionist, she had a good head on her shoulders, and while I found her attractive, She had a keep hands off about her that I respected and could honor.

When I got to the residential hotel, I started up the stairs of the hotel, when a clerk called to me. I had a message.

Lieutenant Sanders had gotten the address for the local National office, along with a note that a Richard Hart would meet me there at two in the afternoon the next day. That worked well for me as my morning was going to be spent with ballistics, a gunsmith and some specialized shopping at the local hardware store. I got into my apartment without any other incidents, however, I still jammed a chair under the doorknob. I pulled down the Murphy bed, got undressed and climbed in for a good night's sleep. Almost twenty-four hours ago I had fallen into the bay and came out cold and soaking wet. Now I was drifting off to sleep and I didn't want a drink.

A Receptionist And A Gun,
Opened For Business

The next morning I arrived at the diner, I went in and took a seat at the counter. Shanna saw me and poured a cup of coffee and brought it to me. This girl had promise. She stopped and just looked at me for a minute and I realized that my coat was opened and she could see the colt. I closed up my coat.

"I have to take it to the precinct today so they can run a ballistics test. I have the cartridges in my pocket, if you want to see." I said.

A voice crept up behind me.

"Just what are you suggesting you show my daughter?" Betty asked.

I turned and paused. She wasn't dressed as a diner cook, but in a business suit. Her auburn hair was up under a smart looking hat, and she sure didn't look like anyone's mother. She was a knockout, but she still had a hands off air about her. She would be perfect for the job as receptionist.

"Uh, nothing," I stammered, I pack, uh carry a colt, I have to take it to take to ballistics, and she saw it..."

"Relax, Mr. Watcher, I heard the whole thing. I have had breakfast, and turned in my notice, so if you have a key for me, I will go up and open the office."

I reached into my pocket and pulled out the keyring and a couple of cartridges. I took the office key off of it and started to hand it to her. Now she was looking in my hand at the bullets.

"I had no idea they were that large," she said. "I have seen thirty-eights at the precinct when I worked there. There is a bit of difference."

I considered making an off-handed remark about mine being bigger, but decided I wasn't prepared for the repercussions that Betty might unleash upon me. Instead, I got to business.

"We'll need new locks for the door and keys that we keep track of. Can you handle that for me?" I asked.

She tilted her head with a look of "Really!". I smiled and dropped the key in her hand and her daughter cleared her throat.

"Coffee."

I turned back around, "Yeah, and steak and eggs and OJ, please. I heard the bell to the diner door as Betty left. The day was starting off okay, I just hoped it would stay that way. Shanna was quick with the breakfast and I was done and off to the precinct to let them play with the colt.

I am positive that the desk sergeant must live behind that desk. I entered and he pointed at a door that said "LAB", they were expecting me.

The lab was impressive. There was a large bay with solid tables and a lot of chemistry stuff placed about. Work stations consisted of partitioned off cubicles. There were several other large walled off cubicles that were identified as to purpose, Fingerprints, Organic Material, Blood Analysis and a couple of others. There were two doors at the other end of the lab, one marked "Morgue", and the other "Ballistics". I had found my destination.

The ballistics lab had a couple of long tables, several unique looking microscopes, a number of guns on the wall and on the counters, some charts of ammunition, and a couple of tanks filled with water. There was also a tank filled with slats and cotton batting. Two men were at the counters and the older one broke away and met me by the door.

"Mr. Watcher, I presume," he said. "I am Dr. Wynant, chief of ballistics, that is Edgar over there, he's a police officer helping me out. They rotate street officers through here as training."

"It's an impressive lab," I said.

"You have the colt?" he asked.

I opened my coat and showed him my gun.

"Take it out with two fingers, please, Edgar over there can be very nervous, no need you getting shot over carelessness." he said.

"I agree," I replied.

I took out the colt and handed it over. Dr Wynant took the colt and examined it. He went through the same process as the Lieutenant in the Discrete office. I wondered who trained who. He held out his hand.

"Bullets, please," he said. He knew the colt

was empty by its weight, I nodded and handed him the three remaining cartridges. He looked at his hand as I dropped them into it. "Is that all you have?"

"That's it."

"I'm afraid I'll use all of these in my tests," he said.

He loaded the gun and walked over to the tank with the cotton batting. He set the gun in a holder and turned to me. "Would you mind flipping that light on the wall behind you?"

I walked over and did as he asked. I turned back and shrugged. Nothing seem to happen.

"It flashes red lights outside of this lab," he said, "it lets everyone know I am about to fire a weapon. Don't want a bunch of police running in here guns blazing, now do we," he smiled.

"Firing, Edgar, three," he said.

He cocked the hammer and pulled the trigger, three times. There were disturbances in the tank marked by cotton batting holders jerking as the bullets passed through. The jerking stopped about half the length of the tank. Edgar walked over to the last batting holder to move and pulled it out. Three blackened marks were in the batting. With gloved hands, Edgar removed the three slugs. Dr, Wynant removed the three shells from the gun and gave them to a waiting Edgar. He took the colt out of the holder and handed it back to me. Then we walked over and he flipped the switch off.

"All clear," he said. "Take your gun and go,

Mr. Watcher. If there are any problems, I am sure Lieutenant Sanders will let you know."

"I am sure he will," I said and I left.

Staying Alive

South of Market was a gunsmith I knew about. Hell Fritz was a gunsmith everyone knew about. Just not like me. I met Fritz in Germany when I was an MP. Because he was a gunsmith he was always under scrutiny. The truth was he was a gifted engineer with a love of the American west. He was a craftsman and when I could do him a favor, I did. Now he had a shop in San Francisco. Not only did I want ammunition, I wanted to be able to switch an unloaded cylinder with a loaded one quickly. Fritz was a man who could make this happen.

The shop door had one of those spring bells that as one entered, rang letting the proprietor know someone was in the front of the shop while he was working in the rear. I hated those bells. A glass counter ran three-quarters of the length of the back of the shop. There were a large number of revolvers, and rifles displayed about the shop, but all were under lock and key.

I stepped up to the counter and placed the colt upon the glass top. A small heavyset man with thinning hair and a full neatly trimmed beard walked from a curtained doorway behind the counter. He was grayer than I remembered, but his eyes still twinkled like he got the joke you missed.

"May I help you," he asked in a slight German accent. "Jonas, Jonas this is you is it not?'

"It is," I said. "How is your family?"

"They are good. And how are you?" he asked.

"Oddly enough I am better."

"You are not with the army any more?" he asked.

"No, I'm not," I said. "We parted company shortly after..."

"Enough," he interrupted. "What can I do for you?"

"I need some ammunition for the colt here and I need some modifications to it."

I opened up the gun and showed him.

"I want to be able to take out a cylinder of spent cartridges and exchange it for one that has loaded cartridges. I need to do it quickly."

I handed Fritz the gun. He examined it carefully.

"This is a nice piece. Hmm single action. You cock and pull the trigger to fire the weapon, but you wish to load it fast?"

He shook his head, then broke the gun down to look at it more carefully.

"There are a number of ways I can do this, but I think the best would be to break the barrel forward, you could slide the cylinder off, and quickly replace it, bring the barrel up and lock it into place. I have done this before, I could have it ready in a couple of days."

I took out a hundred dollars, "Could you have it done any sooner?" I asked.

Fritz scratched his head, and I took out my new temporary PI license and showed it to him.

"You can check with Lieutenant Sanders at the local precinct, he'll vouch for my being a P.I."

"Lieutenant Sanders, what do I care from him, you saved my life."

Fritz reached out and snatched the hundred dollars.

"That and a hundred dollars, gets you ammunition, cylinders, and the weapon ready to be tested this afternoon," he smiled.

I filled out the bill for the work and handed it back to Fritz. I wasn't too happy about traveling around without a weapon, but I knew if I kept my eyes open, I should be okay. As I started to leave Fritz asked me to put up the temporarily closed sign and lock the door as I left.

"And leave my bell alone," he said.

Damn bell.

I wanted to do my shopping, but I decided to see how Betty was getting on at the office and pick up any messages.

There was a locksmith at the door when I arrived. He shifted out of my way as I entered the office, and Betty was getting off the phone. I had two messages, one from Mrs Stanton, and The Lieutenant. Betty silently asked the question.

"Yeah, that Mrs Stanton," I said. "I'm looking for her husband. What did she have to say?"

"She arrived in Los Angeles, and is staying at

the Hollywood Hotel, and wanted to know if you had any news about the case."

"Mrs Stanton sure wants results fast," I said, "Jeez, I just got the case."

This whole thing was surreal to me. I was a bum in a drunk tank less than a week ago. And climbing out of the bay soaked to the skin just the other night, and now I'm a P.I. Looking into a missing man case that may be tied to a murder.

"What did Lieutenant Sanders want?" I asked.

"He called to tell you he appreciated you bringing your weapon down to the precinct so quickly for ballistics. He wants to meet with you after you stop at the National office."

I looked at the workman, "He got here fast," I said. "I can't remember the last time I had someone show up the same morning as I called them."

"It helps that the police have an interest in the place being secure," she replied.

"Look when this guy is done, can you find out what bank we do business with. I have some money to deposit, I'm going to need to have signature cards and stuff like that."

"I'll have the locksmith leave a bill," she said, "we can pay him when I get it worked out."

My head was beginning to spin, there were a lot of little details to be worked out. Betty seemed to have things in hand, so I was off to do some shopping at a hardware store, and I was going to need some new clothes too. Afterward, it was back to Fritz's for my colt.

The hardware store also had one of those springing bells. Jeez. If I had to listen to that all day I would go bonkers. I walked about and picked up some tools and a few odds and ends that would let me create a false bottom in one of the armoires. Also, I wanted to put some detection elements in the apartment. If someone went snooping there, I wanted to know about it. The shopping trip was uneventful and I headed back to my apartment.

The bottom to the armoire on the right side of the Murphy bed was already distressed, so any additional work I did to make the bottom of the armoire the top to a secure box was easy to do. I made it deep enough to hold several folders and my gun and any other odd and ends I wanted to hide. Once I put the floor back in place and pressed in the frame about the inside of the armoire, there was no indication that anything had been done. I put a similar frame into the bottom of the other armoire and locked it down the same as the one with the false bottom. I check the floors of both looking for anything that would indicate that I had done anything to them. Anyone tossing the place would miss the hidden box.

I then turned my attention to the front door. I checked out the hallway to be sure nobody was watching and then I hollowed out a couple spots for warning bits. Small fragments place in the hollows would float gently to the floor when the door was opened and when the door was closed again they would be dispersed by the movement of a closing door. The other warning was clear plastic tape across the lower part to the door. When arriving home if it wasn't intact than someone would have entered the apartment, and may still be there. I added similar elements to the windows, the problem with garden apartments is the windows can provide unwanted access to one's apartment.

Once done with my handy work I took the tools and other things and deposited them in a rubbish bin some blocks from the apartment. I had two appointments in the afternoon, the National office and Fritz. Which I did first depended on my clothes shopping.

I headed to a department store in union square to see what I could find. I wasn't exactly dressed for success. The suit wasn't mine, and it didn't really fit. I looked over several suits of the rack, I was a thirty-eight regular so I figured I could find something. The sales clerks avoided me for a bit and I decided to ask for help. The man closest to me who couldn't get away sighed.

"Yes, sir, can I help you."

"I'm looking for something off the rack in a thirty-eight regular," I said.

I reached in and took out my wallet and opened it slightly.

"You do take cash?" I asked.

"Indeed we do, Sir," he said with more

enthusiasm seeing the bills in my wallet. He proceeded to show me several suits.

By the time I was done, I had two suits, several shirts, socks underwear and two pair of shoes. I spent nearly a hundred dollars and the young man gave me a store card with his name and days he worked in case I needed anything else.

The time took longer than I had expected, I headed back to my apartment My warning device hadn't been triggered. I looked around and since no one was watching I bent down and removed the tape. I removed my other warning so it wouldn't leave a false indicator and I opened the door and went in. I quickly put everything away and got dressed for my appointment with National.

I stopped by the office on my way and it was a good thing I did. The locksmith was gone and Betty was just getting back from lunch and was just opening the door as I exited the elevator. She whistled, I didn't know women whistled.

"You clean up real good, Mr. Watcher. I'm glad you stopped by, I have a key for you and a couple of other things."

We went into the outer office and she pointed to the desk in the inner office. There was a small box on the desk, it was full of business cards, "Discrete Investigations", the address, phone number, no name. She stood in the doorway.

"I hope they will do," she said. "They're blanks that Mickey had on hand. You can get ones with your own moniker, but it takes a couple of days."

I nodded, "These are great, they'll do. I have an appointment with a guy at National, a Richard Hart, we can swap lies while we swap cards."

"A couple more things, you need to go to the bank on the corner, that is where the accounts for the business are. They will open one for you with the business name, but you need to include your own name also, something about Mickey being dead. His accounts are frozen, though as best as I can tell, there isn't much in them. Also a gentleman with a slight German called, he says you should come see him, the work is done. He seemed very pleased with himself."

"His name is Fritz, and he has reason to be pleased with himself," I said.

Betty just nodded. Then she reached into a drawer and pulled out a notebook and a pencil.

"You'll need to take notes with Hart," she said.

I took the notepad and pencil, put them in my pocket and thanked her. Since I was spending a lot of time on my feet, and I was beginning to appreciate the term flatfoot and gumshoe. The new shoes that I was wearing were rubber souled and as I was now walking across damp pavement, if I found myself running wearing leather souled shoes, I would end up on my ass. The funny things one thinks about going from point A to point B.

It was a short walk to the Fritz's, and I opened

the door to that damn ringing bell. Fritz appeared from behind the curtain.

"Ah, you got my message. Turn the open sign in the window to 'return shortly' and lock the door," he said.

I did as he requested.

"Please come through, and let me show you what I have done. I think you will be pleased."

I followed him into the back room. It was a narrow room, with a workbench on one side the entire length of the room. The room was wide enough for a person to work and another to pass without disturbing him. There were three stools placed at different workstations. Fritz didn't always work alone.

There were a number of cubicles above the bench most holding some form of pistol or rifle broken down in parts. The room smelled of gun oil. There were several cutting and drilling tools on the workbench. There were also boxes under the bench with a lot of different raw materials. At the end of the bench against the wall was a bookcase with gun manuals. Fritz could make a gun to order from scratch in here. In front of the bookcase was my colt with three cylinders. There was a doorway at the end of the room.

"Please get your weapon and follow me down to the range and we will see if it suits you."

He reached up into a cubicle and grabbed a box of cartridges and went through. I followed him and discovered a landing and stairs going down. At the bottom was a door which he opened and walked through.

I felt a little bit like Alice in wonderland. On the other side of the door was a two lane range with targets at the opposite end. There were cubicles of a sort to stand in with a bench about chest high to set stuff on. He indicated I take the right one. There was head gear for ear protection hanging on a nail.

"The room is fairly sound proof but the reverberations can be quite strong. I've tested the gun, so I know it won't blow up in your hand."

"Thanks, I appreciate that," I replied

I checked the gun, it was loaded. I put on the head gear, Fritz followed suit and I took aim at the simple circle target at the other end of the room, about fifty feet. I cocked the hammer, and pulled the trigger six times in succession. I paused and looked at the gun. It was different this time, the kick was straighter, maybe it was just the circumstances, but I felt more in control. I slipped off the head gear.

Fritz turned a crank and the target floated back to us. The middle of the target was gone. Fritz tisked and nodded his head.

"You have not lost your skill," he said. "where did you train?"

"In the army," I said.

"I am sorry," he said, "a man should learn to shoot to hunt for food, or for the sport of target shooting, not to kill another man."

58

Fritz replaced the target with a human form target and sent it back down the room. He indicated I give him the gun. I did. He slipped a small metal piece under the cylinder and the barrel dropped away on a small hinge. He jerked the gun lightly and the cylinder dropped into his hand. He put it back, returned the barrel with a slight click. He handed the gun back to me.

"Now you," he said.

I repeated the process and it worked just as simply. He handed me another cylinder and indicated that I do it again. I was not quite as smooth with a second cylinder in my hand, but that would improve with practice.

"Now, you will shoot and do a cylinder switch and shoot again", he said.

I nodded and slipped on the head gear again. I set the used cylinder on the bench and took aim. I cocked the hammer, pulled the trigger six times, I pressed the metal slip, exchanged cylinders a little more smoothly, locked the barrel in place and emptied the gun again. The head to the figure on the target was obliterated, and there was a good size hole in the chest. Fritz brought the target forward.

"Do you want this?" he asked indicating the target.

"No," I said. "Your are right, Fritz, you do excellent work."

"Naturally," he said.

We went back upstairs and reopened his shop.

"And how will you carry it?" asked Fritz.

I was standing there is my suit and holding the colt in my right hand, he was right, I couldn't very well walk down the street with a colt forty-four in my hand, and slipping it into my belt wouldn't work very well. I thought about a shoulder holster, but they didn't make them for colt forty-four's.

"I believe I have a solution to your problem," said Fritz. He reached under the counter and took out a modified shoulder holster. "Take off your coat, and let's see how this fits you."

I set the colt on the counter and slipped off my coat and placed it on the counter, too. He handed me the holster, and I slipped the straps around my shoulders. The holster hung lower and was loose. Fritz then took a clip that fit on the holster and attached to my belt. The holster was high on my waist, but it was firmly against my side. I picked up the forty-four and slid it into the holster. The leather was stiff yet held the colt as if it was made for it.

"You have done this before," I said.

"Of course," he replied.

I put on my coat and went to a mirror at the end of the counter, and looked at myself. I buttoned and unbuttoned my coat several times. The gun and holster didn't interfere with my movements. As I walked and turned the gun held tight to my body. I unbuttoned my coat and reached inside and drew the colt. I wouldn't win any fast draw contests, but the gun pulled free and I was able to shoot unobstructed by the coat.

"I'll take," I said, "how much?"

"It is included," he smiled and nodded.

I looked up at the clock, I had more than enough time to make my appointment with Mr. Hart. I thanked Fritz and headed out the door.

A Puzzle With Too Many Missing Pieces

I flagged down a cab, National was located in a smarter part of town. It was too far to walk, and I wasn't familiar enough yet with the Muni schedule to get where I was going on time. It was then when I realized there was another anomaly to this case.

Why wasn't National working it? They had been instrumental in helping Mrs Stanton reach her husband every other time. Though they never really got eyes on him since New Orleans. What happened in New Orleans? I started to laugh at myself. I had been an MP for the army, and I was in investigations, detective work, but as a shamus on my own, I was in very unfamiliar territory.

I know I survived an ambush on the dock, but that was more luck and reflexes than skill. And though the police think Perfume Eddie was a button man, I think he was just a thug looking to improve on his reputation.

There was something in my office he was determined to get through. Unfortunately he exercised really bad judgment in trying to get it, or was he under some kind of pressure. He must have had a time limit to deliver whatever it was he was looking for. There is also the matter of who sent him. I now knew what my first question for Mr. Hart would be.

The office for the National Investigators

Agency may have been small, personnel-wise, but they took up the whole second floor of the office building they were in. The layout was pretty fancy too. The reception area was bigger than mine, but they had smaller offices off to the side to quickly escort people to after they identified themselves for their appointment.

When I walked in the receptionist was quick to confirm who I was and move me into another office. It was down a hall and on the window side of the building. It was small but comfortable with a couple of overstuffed chairs, a writing table, and a lamp as well as a dimly lit overhead. The artwork on the wall was some kind of nondescript serene landscape. I sat and waited.

The door opened after about five minutes, they were letting me cool my heels and that must have been their stock wait time. I might be new to being a P.I. but I'm familiar with interview techniques.

Hart was a thin man, late twenties, clean shaven about average height in a three piece, full Windsor knotted tie, he had a piece under his coat on his waist, probably a thirty-two. He carried a large notebook, even though he wasn't sure why I was here. He was seeing me as a favor the police department.

"Mr. Watcher, my name is Richard Hart, what can I do for you?" he asked.

I held out my hand, and Hart fumbled with the notebook and put out his hand, I took it but he didn't offer any kind of a grip. Maybe he moonlights as a surgeon. Regardless his hand was clammy. I fought the urge to close down on his hand and simply smiled. After an appropriate time, I withdrew mine and sat down.

Hart looked at me for a moment and took the other chair. I sat back just enough to let the colt shape be apparent. I took out a business card and handed it to Hart. He looked at it and cleared his throat. I wasn't sure how much the police had told Hart, and I wasn't in a giving mood, so I decided I would start with questions and see what I could learn.

"Can you tell me why National is no longer handling the search for Mrs Stanton's husband?" I asked.

"Who say's we aren't?" he stammered.

"Mrs Stanton," I lied.

That hit Hart right between the eyes, and if I ever see him in a poker game, I am going to get in because this man leaves tells all over the place. It meant he was a flunky, or doesn't spend any time in the field. Odd, Lieutenant Sanders sent me to Hart specifically. Was Hart more likely to give me information, or was he so low on the totem pole, that interviewing him wouldn't raise any red flags? I decided to push a little more and see what I could get.

"I have Mrs Stanton's version, but maybe you can give me National's response to why she was unhappy," I pressed.

"Unhappy, uh, I suppose the events in..."

He was temporizing, so I knew I was on the right track.

"In New Orleans, yeah, you were there, right," I finished.

I thought Hart might wet himself, but he took a couple of breaths and started his monologue, it's amazing what a few well placed words can accomplish.

"I am not a field agent," Hart said in a loud whisper trying not to blurt it out. He took a deep breath. "I am a forensics accountant."

"What, you're a CPA for dead people?" I asked.

Hart was taken aback and he smiled at the humor in my question. He relaxed and went into education mode, which was fine with me. I leaned forward and took out my notebook and pencil, this was going to be more informative than I had hoped.

"How is forensics accounting involved with the Stanton case?" I asked.

"Initially it wasn't, when Martin. Stanton went missing, the first time, two operatives were assigned the case to locate him."

"Who were they?"

"William Mason and Sam Parrish. They worked out of the New York office. They contacted the various offices and put out a flier on him. The Miami office responded very quickly with where he was. Mrs Stanton went down with

Mason and Parrish. They returned to New York, Mrs Stanton stayed in Miami, and that seemed to be the end of things. Mrs Stanton spent about a month with her husband in Miami, a second honeymoon maybe.

"Anyway she eventually returned to New York. He stayed in Miami. She set him up with a studio and a monthly allowance of a grand."

I whistled

"He was there for a while, he painted and kept a pretty low profile. He had a couple of local art shows, actually sold some paintings. Then gone."

"So how does an accountant get involved?" I asked.

"I getting to that. Mason and Parrish were brought in again, and they pretty much followed the same pattern for searching for him. They weren't having as much luck when the head of National put out a request for ideas. I had just started in the San Francisco office. We do more accounting detective work here."

"Auditing, looking for embezzlers," I said.

"Very good, Mr. Watcher. Not many people know that financial crime is bigger than most other crimes monetarily."

I didn't either, but I was learning.

"Go on, Mr. Hart," I encouraged him.

"With Mrs Stanton's help, I knew we had some financial information on her husband. His bank account, credit use, property owned and any financial activities. His savings and checking accounts provided most of the information needed to track his movements. He also had an odd need to make credit purchases, and this was also helpful.

"With that information, I was able to discover that he was doing business in St Louis and New Orleans, but mostly St Louis. National doesn't have an office in St Louis, so it was assigned to Chicago. But that office dispatched Mason and Parrish from New York. Within a couple of weeks, they reported back that he was in New Orleans, but we couldn't physically locate him."

"Why Mason and Parrish?" I asked.

"They were familiar with the case. They felt that it was their case, and they convinced the boss in Chicago to let them find him. They went to New Orleans and it seemed they were successful in contacting Martin Stanton. Then, poof he disappeared like an erased line item. They were returned to New York and were assigned to another case."

"How did they find out he went to Los Angeles?" I asked.

"Martin Stanton contacted his wife directly. She got a post office box from her husband and she continued to send money to him. National was taken out of the loop."

Hart paused, and I knew something was wrong. I looked around and I didn't see anyone or thing to bother about, but Hart was thinking, too hard. I was starting to like the kid, but I wasn't sure what his look was about. He was conflicted. He was looking at the lamp. Overhead light and a lamp. I folded over a page in my notebook and wrote down one word, and I showed it to him. The word was "bugged".

He nodded.

I knew the story changed in New Orleans, but the kid was scared, so I decided we needed a change of venue. All of this happened very quickly so I temporized for a moment.

"Thanks for letting me catch up on my note taking, Mr. Hart," I said. "I see the repetitive nature of all of this. I got Mr. Stanton must be in San Francisco somewhere, and I think Mrs Stanton just wants to make sure he continues getting his checks. Thanks for your time."

While talking I made several notes and showed them to Hart. The first "was anyone listening now?" he shook his head, "No".

Next I wrote, "We need to talk somewhere more private." He nodded with enthusiasm.

We stood up and shook hands, his was less limp this time, and not so clammy. We exited the small room, and he said, "I'll walk you out, Mr. Watcher, I have some personal business to take care of."

He turned to the receptionist, " Jennifer, I have to go out, I won't be back until tomorrow morning".

Then to me, "Wait for me at the elevator, Mr. Watcher, and I'll go down with you."

I walked to the elevator, I unbuttoned my coat and stood so I could see all exits, just in case. Richard Hart came out of the office and we entered the elevator.

"I hope I have not made a mistake with you, Mr. Watcher." he said.

"If it is worth anything, Lieutenant Sanders will vouch for me," I said.

He nodded. I suggested we take a cab and go to my office.

"Oh, no, that won't do," he said, "I'm sure it is being watched."

"How about a gun-shop south of Market," I said.

"Excellent, there is no notation in the file of your going there," he said.

" What about Marlon Apartments?"

"No," he said, "you have been seen entering a diner in the same building as Mickey Philips office, the police station, and of course the office itself. No one has been tailing you as yet."

When we entered the gun-shop, same stupid bell, and Fritz entering from the back room.

"Is there something wrong with the gun?" he asked.

"No Fritz, I need a less public place to continue a discussion with Mr. Hart, here."

"But, of course, my back room is at your disposal, I can busy myself out here. Do I need..."

"I think we are okay, but sitting with a little

69

fire power at quick reach might be advisable," I said.

Fritz merely smiled and nodded. As we entered the back room, Fritz sat on a stool at the end of the counter away from the door with cover and what appeared to be a small arsenal within easy reach.

We both sat down on stools facing each other.

"So what happened in New Orleans?" I asked.

"I need to back up a bit," he said. "Mason and Parrish, were on a case and they went to New Orleans, even though I suggested the financial trail was in St Louis. It should have been a simple contact and forward information, but it seemed to last for a month or more. Then Mr. Stanton vanishes from New Orleans. The problem is that my data indicated that Martin Stanton was in St Louis more than he was in New Orleans. But Mason and Parrish insist he was in New Orleans.

" While they're there, some guy they were trying to get information from does a swan dive off some bridge under construction in New Orleans. Mason and Parrish contact both the Chicago and New York Office, they have sighted Stanton in New Orleans. They play cat and mouse with him for a couple of weeks, and they supposedly corner him and he agrees to communicate with Mrs Stanton, but he doesn't want to see her. He telegrams her directly and he talks with her on the phone for a couple times and they set up the same arrangement.

"While this is going on, Stockard and Mason return to New York. Parrish quits National and heads back to New Orleans. Then Stanton takes off for Los Angeles, but this time he gives Mrs Stanton a forwarding address."

"Any chance it isn't Stanton," I asked.

"Mrs Stanton says it is him. He is even thinking of returning to New York and to the art scene there, but he has some business in Los Angeles."

"Mason thinks something is wrong and wants to follow him to Los Angeles, but the Boss says Mrs Stanton is okay with things. Mason gets pissed and quits, and disappears."

"What aren't you telling me here?" I asked.

"Two things that seem unrelated. The guy running a successful office in Chicago requests a transfer to run San Francisco. I like San Francisco, but we mostly do accounting stuff, the Chicago office is three floors, twenty-five agents, and they're into everything. How come Steven Jaxom wants to come to San Francisco?"

"And the second thing?"

"I was still doing some forensics accounting on Mr. Stanton. There was stuff going on in New Orleans, but not quite enough, and there was a lot more going on in St Louis. Banking, credit, and property transfers, it was like he was in two different places at once. Initially, I thought he was traveling back and forth between the two cities and I sort of dropped it because there was no active case. But when he contacted Mrs Stanton from New Orleans that he was going to Los Angeles, my data indicators were he was in St Louis.

"When he went to LA, everything checked out, he rented an apartment and he was seen by a couple of people and he seemed fine. But when I looked back at the financial activity, just before he went to Los Angeles There was a lot of it. In fact he was liquidating stuff, it looked like he was getting ready to leave the country. Stuff showed up in Los Angeles, but it didn't fit with what was liquidated."

"So what did you do?"

"I told the Boss in New York, but he thought I was putting too much emphasis on the numbers. And besides we were off the case. So I called Mickey Philips, I had met him before, I told him what I had. He contacted Mrs Stanton, and told her there might be some irregularities, and could he have a copy of the National file on her husband. He said he was going to do some work on speck. He asked me for my file information, so I sent it to him."

"Why aren't you dead?" I asked.

Hart looked at me with a shocked expression. "What do you mean, dead?" he asked.

"Look, kid," I said, "you may well have put two guys in the frame and another hovering around it. If what you have just told me is close to the truth, it may well be what got Mickey Philips killed. So how come you are still walking around? Where is your boss?"

"Mr. Jaxom, he's in Sacramento on an unrelated case. Some kind of land swindle. I haven't been filing reports after the Boss said we were off the case. But I hadn't sent my report to Mr, Philips until after he left for Sacramento. It should be in Philips' office mail."

There hadn't been any mail in the office, which means Philips either had a P.O. box or he had his mail held until he got back from Sacramento. Why did he go to Sacramento? Why was Jaxom really there? I don't believe in coincidences.

"Who went to Sacramento first, Philips or Jaxom?" I asked.

Hart shrugged, he didn't know. I had to get to the Discrete's office and fast, also I needed to put Hart on ice for awhile. Can't let the police know about him just yet, I have a feeling something is not quite right, either in Sacramento or here. I decided to put him up in my place, it's not on anyone's map just yet, so it would be the safest place for him. I gave him my keys and directions to my apartment. I told him no phone calls except to call my office, and he was only to talk to me or my receptionist. Let either of us know if there's anything he needs.

"Oh, yeah, if a man answers, and it isn't me, hang up! Then sit tight."

"Do you really think I am in danger?" he

asked.

I gave him the look that said, really. Then he took the keys and headed for the door.

"Kid, no side trips, if you are in danger, if someone is looking for you..."

"I have had some training, I'll watch for tails, straight to your place." And he was gone.

I felt bad sending him off by himself, but Betty was in the office and there might be some real danger there. When I got to the office building, I went up the stairs. I waited by the fourth floor stairway entrance to catch my breath. If I was really going to be doing this I needed to get in better shape. I opened the door a crack, and when no one appeared to be in the hallway I headed for the office. I opened the door and all seemed to be okay, Betty looked up and smiled.

"Been to the bank yet?" she asked.

"No, I'll do it tomorrow. Any calls?" I asked

"Mrs Stanton, she is back in San Francisco, she's at The Palace, wants you to stop by. Also, Lieutenant Sanders, says you should stick around, he wants to talk, about a couple of things."

"Anything else?"

""I got the mail that had been on hold, delivered. They complained, but I told them the police wanted the mail delivered today."

I looked in the inner office, there was a small stack on the desk, I could see the large envelope with Hart's report in it. I unbuttoned my coat. Betty watched me.

"We expecting trouble?" she asked.

"Maybe. You afraid of guns?" I asked.

"If that's a cute way of asking if I can shoot, yes I can. I was on the force, and although their policy is women do not carry, I had a boss who wanted everyone to know how to shoot."

Just then the phone rang, I motioned for Betty to let me pick up.

"Watcher," I said.

It was Hart, he had got to my place without incident. He was hungry and wanted some magazines, and the evening paper. I described Betty and told him she would stop by in a little while. I hung up.

"Mr. Hart is at my place," I said writing down my address on the back of a business card. "I need you to deliver him something from the diner, burger fries and some kind of soft drink, No booze, he needs to keep all his faculties. He wants some reading material, paper and some weekly's. Then go home, you're good for the day."

"Okay if I have dinner with my daughter?"

"Works for me," I said. I handed her a double sawbuck. "Tomorrow before you come in, stop by Fritz's, he's a gunsmith, south of Market."

"I know the place," she said.

"He's a friend, he'll give you a piece for the office, tell him you want him to set up a holder behind the vanity panel of your desk."

"You didn't tell me the job was dangerous,"

she said.

"Dead guy on my first day, old owner dead, you're kidding, right?"

She put on her coat and hat. And started for the door.

"I'll keep and eye out, don't worry, I'll be okay." She locked the door when she left.

What It's Like To Play The Palace

I headed into the office to grabbed that report from Hart, I wanted a closer look. Betty had coffee on the hot plate, I poured myself a cup and turned off the plate. The coffee smelled good, and surprisingly tasted liked it smelled. The mail consisted mostly of advertising, bills, and...

I opened the report and settled behind the desk in the cushy chair. Most of it went over my head, but Hart's notes were very complete, and by the time I had gotten to the end I had an interesting picture of Martin Stanton's movements, and while some things didn't add up, one thing was for sure. Martin Stanton died in New Orleans.

There was a knock at the door, and I got up to answer it, using my left hand to open the door while having my right hand on the butt of my colt. In the course of the last twenty-four hours, it had gone from being someone else's gun in a running bag, to being mine. It was Lieutenant Sanders at the door. He peered at me cautiously.

"You expecting unwanted company?" he asked.

"No, just being cautious," I replied.

I closed and locked the door behind him. He looked back at the door and shrugged. I invited him into my office and offered him a cup of coffee. He accepted. I sat down behind the desk and he took a client chair and put his feet up on the desk.

"You've been busy, today," he said.

"Picked up some clothes, had my colt worked on, hired a receptionist, talked to Richard Hart, got the mail, and determined Martin Stanton is dead. My best guess is he was killed in New Orleans."

Sanders stopped in mid sip of his coffee, he didn't seem too surprised, but he wanted more information.

"Two questions Sherlock, what did you do to the Colt, and just how the hell did you come to the conclusion that Stanton is dead.?"

I figured Sanders was more interested in how I deduced that Stanton was dead, but I decided to answer his first question before I went over Hart's report. I took out the Colt and opened it showing him how, and removed the cylinder. I put the cylinder back and closed the gun. I handed it across the desk butt first. Sanders took it, he slipped out the cartridges one by one and put them on the desk. He twirled it a couple of times. He opened the gun and pulled off the cylinder and looked at the gun examining Fritz's workmanship. He smiled and handed it back to me after reloading it and closing the gun up.

"No loss of balance, and quick to reload. Not bad. How the hell did you determine Stanton is dead, and is there any proof?" he asked.

"No proof as of yet," I said. "Hart is an impressive forensic's accountant. He was able to show Stanton traveling from New York to Miami.

And according to his notes Stanton was preparing to leave the country, but something changed his mind and he headed for St Louis"

"I thought he went to New Orleans?"

"That is what the report from National said, but if you remember, Mrs Stanton had no direct contact with Martin in person after Miami."

I paused and leaned back in my chair and put my feet on the desk. I interlaced my fingers behind my head and continued.

"All the contact was between William Mason or Sam Parrish. The same William Mason who was recently hired by Mickey Philips."

"How did you put all this together, a couple of days ago you were a drunk on the wharf?" asked the Lieutenant.

"My job as an MP was in investigations. While we were trying to extricate ourselves out of Europe after the war, we had a number of, shall we say people who were looking to make a killing off the confusion of what was going on. My job was to minimize it. When I mustered out, there was a depression going on, and at the time the only people looking for someone with my talents, I didn't want to work for. Let's leave it at that."

"And now?" he asked.

"Survival," I replied. "I got knocked into the bay and was lucky not to have drown. I have a strange feeling that my ending up here was not in someone's master plan."

The Lieutenant took his feet off the desk and

stood up and I joined him.

"I figure that either you're full of it, or you're on the level," said the lieutenant, "and, to be honest, I don't care which. I wasn't a big fan of Philips. He was a little bent, with just enough integrity. He was a good resource, and he didn't deserve being killed in Sacramento."

"Keep digging, Watcher," said the Lieutenant, then he laughed. "Just remember, I'm watching you. I'll lock up on my way out."

The Lieutenant left and I stayed in my office for a couple of minutes, then I checked the outer door, he did lock it. So far so good. The phone rang and I went to answer it. Mrs Stanton.

"Hello, Mrs Stanton," I said after she identified herself. "If you are looking for an update, why don't you drop by the office tomorrow, and..."

"No, No, Mr. Watcher, I actually need your services tonight," she said.

"Tonight?"

"Yes I am to attend an artist showing at The Palace in the main room, and I cannot arrive unattended, and Joseph simply will not do. There is a buffet, and you only need to be near in case I need rescuing from anyone really boring. Please, Mr. Watcher, you can update me during lulls in the showing."

I actually had ulterior motives in going to The Palace, so I told Mrs Stanton that I would be there in about an hour. That was fine with her.

"I hope it is business casual," I said, "I won't have time to change to black tie."

"That is fine, Mr. Watcher, I will see you in an hour."

"The Palace was fifteen minutes away, and I wanted to do some reconnaissance, before I escorted her to the art showing."

I collected some photo's from the National report that I wanted to show to some people. Something still bothered me about the whole Stanton case. There were too many unknowns and they seemed to multiply with the more I learned. I didn't remember cases in Europe getting this complicated unless someone was deliberately making them so.

I checked the colt and dropped the extra cylinders into a coat pocket. It seemed silly, but usually when I figured things were going to be quiet, just the opposite happened, and I wanted to be prepared. I turned out the lights and double checked the door was locked as I left. I took the elevator down with my coat unbuttoned. As I exited the lobby I buttoned my coat and felt a little foolish as I stepped out on to the sidewalk. After a couple of moments I was able to hail a cab and I climbed in telling the driver to take me to The Palace.

A habit I picked up in Europe was to watch the rear view mirror for a couple of minutes after I got in a cab. It was so automatic that I almost ignored the car that pulled out from the curb, right after my cab did. I decided to check if I was being paranoid.

"Driver, there is a news stand just up the way here, on the right, would you stop while I pick up a paper."

"Sure, Mac," he said.

We pulled over and I got out. I paused deciding which paper to pick up. I turned and looked up as if I had heard something. Whoever he was, tailing someone wasn't one of his skills. I picked up a paper, paid for it, and jumped back into the cab and told the driver to continue to The Palace. He did.

After a minute or so, the cabbie spoke up. "Hey, Mac, you know we're being followed?"

"Yeah," I said.

"You want me to lose him?" he asked.

"Nah. Actually do your best not to lose him, but don't let him know we're on to him."

"You got it, Mac."

The drive through San Francisco traffic was fairly light and the driver paced himself so that the car following us was able to stay up through lights. I didn't want to look back to let my tail know I was on to him.

"Can you keep an eye out and give me any information about the person following me?" I asked.

"People," he said. "There are two of 'em. Driving a black Buick. They both smoke."

Clearly the cabbie had done this sort of thing before. As he drove he kept his calm. Driving through San Francisco streets is no small task, especially while giving me a running description when he had any new information.

The men were in trench coats and they both wore hats. Basic body type was average on both of them. By the time my cab pulled up to The Palace, I had pretty good descriptions of my shadows.

I got out. My tail hung back. I paid through the front passenger window so I could get a better look. I gave the cabbie a generous tip and my card and asked him to call me. I also got his card and cab information so I could ask for him specifically.

"Unless this is not something you want to go through again."

The Cabbie smiled, "Are you kidding, this is the best ride I've had in some time. You tip real good too, you need a cab, you call me, ask for Max."

I stood up and smiled. The Buick pulled past and the driver was clearly looking for a place to park. They were not going away. I continued to be the bait and I was slow in going into the lobby, and I was worried because my two tails were still looking for a parking place when one of them finally figured out, that they could separate. I hoped I hadn't been too obvious about knowing they were following me.

I stayed to the center of the lobby looking as

if I was trying to get my bearings, which wasn't too difficult, because I was. Towards the back and off to the side was as very elegant shoe shine seating area next to a barber shop, and it was an excellent place to keep an eye on who came into the lobby. I was a half hour early for my "date" with Mrs Stanton, so I'd get as much as I could on my two admirers before meeting up with her.

I headed for the shoe shine area, I wasn't too sure what to call it, three raised lounge seats in a wooden mahogany base that stood next to the door of an in hotel barber shop, and that isn't an apt description either. A black man in a kind of footman uniform bearing the Palace emblem was finishing up with a man's shoes. The man paid and stepped down.

"Do I need an appointment?" I asked.

The black man stood up and grinned at me. "No Suh, you do not, not with Billie Whitehall," he said in a rich Jamaican accent. "Step on up and get a shine."

I climbed up on a seat, though it would be better described as a lounge chair. I placed my feet on to the foot rest, and sat back.

"Give me your best shine," I said.

Billie gave a small twist of his head and looked at me closely. "That is some weight your packing, sir, do I need to be concerned about anything," he said, his rich accent softened considerably.

"Weight?" I asked.

"If you don't mind me saying, where it is sitting at your side, it ain't no thirty-two or thirty-eight. I make it a forty-four or bigger."

Billie continued his shine without missing a beat.

I sat holding a paper as if I was casually looking at it while I kept an eye on the main lobby door. "I have a license," I said, "But to answer your question, everything should be cool for now."

"Yeah, but you keep watching that door as if you're expecting someone."

I looked down at Billie Whitehall and suddenly realized he could be a major asset. "Billie, would you be interested in a proposition?"

"I don't mix in anything illegal, or that might get me shot. Promised the Missus."

"Actually, I don't want you to do anything you don't normally do. Just keep your eyes and ears open, and upon occasion collect information for me."

"I gotta go anywhere?" he asked.

"Nope just stay here, shine shoes, and if anything odd occurs, let me know."

"An' what is this worth to you?"

"Twenty a week, every week rain or shine," I said

"Just who are you?"

'I'm a private investigator..."

"You are the man who took out Perfume

Eddie," Said Billie as he straightened up a bit.

I looked surprised.

"San Francisco is a small city," he said.

"Is that a problem?" I asked

Billie laughed, "Hell no, he was a piece of shit, but it took some skill to take him out, he wasn't no slouch. And that is a forty-four your packing. Why you want me?"

"You're invisible, Billie, I mean no disrespect, all service people are invisible. You're a part of the furniture, you can listen while doing your job and people ignore you."

"They do that."

"You interested?"

"When do I start?" he asked.

He snapped the cloth he was buffing my shoes with and straightened up. My two tails entered the lobby and I casually pointed them out.

"I picked them up outside my office. Just let me know where they are when I return. I have an engagement with Mrs Stanton," I said.

Billie whistled, "That's nice work, you escorting her to the Art shindig in the Grand Ballroom?"

"I guess I am," I said.

I handed him a little over twenty bucks and said it was his retainer, plus the shoeshine.

"It will be nice working for you, uh,"

"Watcher, Jonas Watcher," I said as I slipped him my card along with the money. Billie nodded and waited for another patron.

The Palace: Act II

I headed for the front desk, and my shadows hung back on the fringe, clearly they were supposed to watch me, then I wondered if one of the Fickle Bitches might not have other plans.

As I approached the check-in area, the clerk behind the "Desk" was quick to step forward to see what I wanted.

"May I help you, Sir?" he asked.

"My name is Jonas Watcher, and I am here to see Mrs Stanton," I said.

"Is she expecting you?" he asked.

I didn't think someone could snub and look down on you with such a simple phrase.

"If you check, you will see that she is. I am surprised that you don't already know," I replied. Two could play this game, and I was older and bigger. "Don't stand there gaping, surely you intend to announce me." Maybe I was rubbing it in a little thick, Nah.

The clerk picked up the phone and called her room, I couldn't quite hear him but apparently Mrs Stanton was better at the game than I. The young man was sheepishly apologetic and directed me to the elevators and quietly repeated her suite number to ensure I got it.

"Thank you," I replied with a little less ice then before.

When I entered the elevator, the young man asked me for my floor.

"The clerk at the front desk told me to ask for the penthouse, Mrs Stanton's suite," I said.

"You must be Mr. Watcher," he said.

He didn't wait for anyone else to enter the elevator. He closed the door and turned a key marked with a capital "P". The ride was a lot smoother than the one in my building. The young man opened the door and pointed to the left. "Suite 'A'," he said.

I stepped off the elevator, but he waited. I guess we were going back down, I thought. When I arrived at the door, it was opened by a man in a formal butler attire.

"Mr. Watcher for Mrs Stanton," I said trying not to sound pompous.

"Yes, Sir," he replied "You're expected. Please come in. Madam will be out shortly. If you would go into the sitting room."

This was the first hotel room I entered that had an entry. Clearly this is not a six bit room. The sitting room was not huge, but it was bigger than my office. I chose to stand by the window rather than sit down, I wasn't sure which was proper, or even if there was a proper. Mrs Stanton was prompt as she entered. No butler with her, no Joseph either. While I was concerned about my dress for the occasion, after seeing Mrs Stanton, I didn't feel overdressed. She was wearing a calf length fitted number that cut to leave something to the imagination both above and at the hem, but the back was slit to let her walk comfortably. While the front of the dress was modest the back was low enough to cause a man's mind to wonder, but not too far.

"Would you like something to drink, Mr. Watcher?" she asked.

"Club soda, would be good.," I said. "On duty so to speak."

She pouted a bit, but pushed a button on a table and the butler appeared.

"A Manhattan for me," she said, "and a club soda for Mr. Watcher."

"Yes Ma'am," the butler said.

"Shall we sit," she said.

She moved to a couple of chairs in a corner by the window and I followed. I held the chair for her and noticed that in the other room Joseph was seated by a bar eating a sandwich. Not far from his employer. By the way he was consuming the sandwich, I understood why he wouldn't do. I sat down next to her and the butler entered with our drinks. I started to speak, but she gestured that I take my drink first.

"A toast," she said.

The butler left.

"Sorry about that," she said, "I don't know him, so I would just as soon as keep my business from being ease dropped upon."

I nodded.

"So, Mr. Watcher, just what have you found out?' she asked.

I decided not to tell her I thought her husband was dead, after all I had no real proof, but I wanted her to believe I was making progress in finding his where abouts.

"I enlisted the help of a National operative to get some additional information about your husband's movements," I said.

Her's eyes widened for a brief moment, she was afraid of that. I decided to calm any fears she had.

"This was old information on your husband," I said, "but it might be useful. The operative is more of an accountant than an investigator. Kind of a mousy guy.

"With the information he gave me, I was able to trace your husband to Los Angeles and then up here to San Francisco. I don't have a lock on his current where abouts, but I have a better track on him then I had before."

She sipped at her Manhattan while I told her about my interview with Mr. Hart though it was pretty much all fiction to this point. I watched her tells as I elaborated on my yarn to see if there were any areas where she might have knowledge.

Hart being an accountant was disturbing to her, so I avoided the fact he was a forensics accountant. She was more relaxed when the information he provided to me was more about her husband leaving a financial trail. When I finished, she downed the last of her drink and stood up, so I did too.

"The art function is in the Grand Ballroom. It shouldn't be more than a couple of hours. So if you would escort me, I would be forever in your debt," she said.

"My pleasure," I replied.

She went to get a wrap, and I noticed that Joseph had left half a second sandwich and half a beer on the bar where he was eating. Maybe he was done. I wondered what the Fate Sisters had in store for me now. Fickle bitches.

Mrs Stanton returned, we left the apartment and took the elevator down to the Grand Ballroom.

As we entered the lobby I spotted Billie Whitehall and it was clear he wanted to talk to me. I couldn't break from Mrs Stanton immediately. I acknowledged his signal and continued to escort Mrs Stanton to the Grand Ballroom. I indicated I would meet him by the barbershop in about ten minutes.

The Grand Ballroom was impressive, high vaulted ceilings, yet the acoustics were excellent. There was a large crowd of people meandering and talking and yet the din was not intrusive. The one side was separated from the other by brass poles attached with thick velvet ropes.

There was a walkway from the buffet to where the artwork was hung. They didn't want food in the gallery area. At one end was a full bar handing out free drinks. I picked a hell of a time to stay sober.

Mrs Stanton stopped to talk to a number of people, introducing me as a family friend. It was easy to determine who believed I was a family friend or her nights entertainment. It didn't matter to me which and I responded appropriately to whatever comments were made.

The only hiccup occurred when we were confronted by a couple of men who had truly taken too much advantage of the open bar. Even the very rich have their drunks. One insisted that he and Mrs Stanton were old friends and surely she would join him in a celebratory drink. They must have been cut off at the bar and had hoped to get the hostess to provide them with more liquor.

We were near a couple of chairs and a well place foot in the back of a knee allowed me to seat one of the gentlemen. Mrs Stanton simply raised up on the ball of her foot, turned and brought her heel down on the foot of the second inebriate. He cried out and I escorted him to the other chair.

"Cramp," I said, to a concerned couple. "An old football injury acting up."

We continued to move through the crowd. Mrs Stanton thanked me for handling it with some finesse. As we approached the buffet I pulled her aside.

"I have been contacted by an operative," I said, "and I need to check in with him. This could mean that there is news."

"Of course," she replied, "enough people have seen you arrive with me, that I shouldn't be bothered by anyone. Please do return as soon as you can. I will be in the gallery when you get back."

I made my way quickly to the lobby and headed for the barber shop. Billie Whitehall was waiting by the door, he handed me an envelope. I took it and opened it, there was a folded up piece of paper inside. I opened it up, it was blank.

"Quietly," he said, "You should be reading that, while I talk to you. You meeting a black man and jawing, would raise eyebrows, but if I hand you a letter waiting for a reply, that won't turn any heads."

I continued staring at the blank piece of paper with a slight smirk. He could be over thinking this, but I appreciated his carefulness.

"What have you got," I asked.

"Not a lot, your two shadows hung about in the lobby sticking out like a couple of sore thumbs. Whatever that may be, private techs, they are not. I was going to give up on them when they were joined by a third man."

"Is he still here?" I asked.

"Nope, and neither are they. I walked over with a small ashtray and sifted butts out of the sand near them. You are right I am invisible, never knew it could be valuable."

"Don't let it go to your head," I said, "you're not getting paid enough to risk your neck."

"This third man was real excited, said something about a heart. Then he said they were to go to some apartment place he would show them and grab something. He also wanted them to toss your office and find some report about Mrs Stanton. Anyway when he was done they split, just a little before you came down."

"This third man, you ever see him before?" I asked.

"Mrs Stanton's chauffeur," he said.

"Shit!"

"Not here you don't."

"I need you to do me two favors," I said. I took out the cabbies card and handed it to Billie. "Call his dispatch and tell him that I need him, now. It's worth fifty to me."

"You sure as hell are going to play havoc with the economy around here. I ain't complaining mind you."

"Second, call Lieutenant Sanders," I gave him Sander's card, " and tell him to meet me at my apartment, things suddenly got very hot and we may need to avoid another murder."

"Mm mm mm," said Billie, "This morning I didn't expect to be involved in all this."

"You're not," I replied "and I intend it to stay that way, it is the only way you stay valuable"

"Yes, Sir, but it makes for a nice story for the Missus, she thinks I live a dull life. I'll get on these calls."

We departed company, and I headed back to the ballroom. Mrs Stanton was going to have to cut her social agenda short for the night. I said something, and now even Mrs Stanton might be in danger. She was on the art show side of the Grand Ballroom talking to a couple dressed to the nines. I approached quietly to confirm they were engaged in small talk and then I interrupted.

"Excuse me, Mrs Stanton, but I need a moment of your time. There has been a development that needs your attention."

The couple looked at Mrs Stanton, exploding with curiosity, but clearly they were not in her confidence, as she courteously excused herself, but in such a manner as to let the couple know this was not to be a subject of further conversation. I guided her to a corner that I could observe anyone approaching while talking to her in confidence.

"You will need to cut your evening short," I said. "There has been a disturbing development, that indicates that you may be in danger."

"Don't be ridiculous," she said. "Why should I be in danger?"

I paused and looked at her for several moments, and decided to lay out the short version for her.

"There is evidence that your husband has been murdered, and you may be on the killer's list"

She stared opened mouthed at me trying to assimilate it all. The one thing that wasn't in her face was grief. That answered one question for me, but the possibility of his being dead was news to her, so I was fairly sure she wasn't involved in his being killed. The other thing her expression confirmed; she was suspicious he might be dead. I did not have time to explore what all this meant just now, because I needed to get to my apartment to keep Hart alive.

I took her up to her apartment, confirmed Joseph wasn't present. I convinced the butler that Mrs Stanton was in danger, and the source was the chauffeur. That didn't surprise Mrs Stanton at all. I was missing something, and I wasn't sure if Hart had the missing pieces or not, and I need to get to him now.

As I exited the elevator Billie Whitehall was in the lobby and handed me a note as he indicated the cab was here. I hurried out the door and read the brief note. Lieutenant Sanders would meet me in front of my apartment. I stepped into the cab and told Max to go to my apartment and step on it, I would cover any tickets.

This late at night the streets were lightly traveled by other vehicles, and I discovered that Max knew a few shortcuts that shortened the distance traveled to my place which consisted going down one way streets the wrong way.

Shots Fired, Three Men Down

When we got to my apartment building, Lieutenant Sanders was waiting outside. I handed Max a sawbuck and told him to get lost, fast. I searched up and down the street for the car that had been tailing me earlier. I didn't see it. It meant one of two things, they hadn't gotten here yet, or they took a different vehicle, but I didn't see anyone on the street that resembled the two mokes following me. The Lieutenant approached me looking around also.

"You expecting visitors?" he asked.

"That is why you are here," I said. "There are two possibly three gentlemen interested in Mr. Hart's health."

"They want him healthy?" he asked.

"More likely they want to be the cause of his sudden death," I replied.

We turned and entered the lobby of the residential hotel, I opened my coat and pulled out my revolver. I carried it at my side, cocking the hammer. The hotel was quiet and the click echoed. The Lieutenant put his hand on his gun, but he kept it holstered for the time being. He felt more secure than I did. The night manager looked up from his newspaper and slowly closed it and started to reach for the phone. The Lieutenant flashed his badge and the manager put the phone back down. He slid down in his chair and moved it out of sight. I looked up at the stairs, they were empty, the elevator door was closed and it wasn't running. We headed for the stairs.

The trip up to the second floor was uneventful, but something didn't seem quite right. We started down the hall, passed the elevator, and arrived at my room. I knocked on the door.

"Hey, Hart, it's Watcher and Lieutenant Sanders, go ahead and open up," I said.

"What's the password, " he said from the other side.

"There isn't any stupid password, you idiot," I said.

The lock clicked and Hart yelled out, "The guy earlier didn't know that!"

The elevator door was closed on the main floor, that's what was wrong! If the elevator wasn't running, it should have been on the main floor and the door should have been opened. That meant it was being held on another floor! I kicked the door to the apartment open knocking Hart back onto his ass. I grabbed Lieutenant Sanders by the arm and pulled him into the room as the first sounds of gunshots echoed in the hallway. Sanders swore in pain as we cleared the doorway. I swung him towards the bed, turned and faced the door raising the colt.

The first man was quick to get into the room, as he filled the doorway I aimed at the middle of his chest I pulled the trigger. His face showed surprise as the slug tore into his chest and sent him backwards into the hall.

A second man was stopped outside the door and started to swing his gun in and start firing. From behind me, I could hear Sanders swearing as he fired several shots from his automatic. That caused the second shooter to throw himself back against the wall just outside the door. It was his second mistake, I cocked the hammer and pulled the trigger of the colt three times, aiming at the wall the man was hiding behind. When he realized what I was doing, Lieutenant Sanders followed suit. The thud from outside the room confirmed the second shooter was down. I broke open the colt and exchanged cylinders.

I looked back at Sanders as he stood up, he was bleeding from his left arm, but he seemed okay.

"There's a third shooter," he whispered, "started out of the closet in the hall, he still has to be there, we're between him and a clean exit."

He moved to the side of the doorway, and I joined him.

"Let's make him run," I said quietly.

"There's another shooter on the right!" I yelled.

"Let's jump out and fill the hallway with lead," Sanders shouted.

Our quarry yelled "Shit!" out in the hallway, and he ran passed the doorway. It was the chauffeur, Joseph.

I stepped out as he was running for the stairs

and aimed high on his back."

"Alive, if you please," said Sanders.

I lowered my colt.

"Right cheek," he said.

I took aim and fired once, it was enough. It caught the man and spun him and he lost his footing, falling down at the head of the stairs. He dropped his gun. I stepped quickly over him and cocked the hammer. He turned and looked at me, then he looked at his gun. He started reaching for it.

"I wouldn't do that if I was you," I said.

"You've only got six shots in that thing, you haven't had time to reload," he replied.

"You take a real good look at the cylinder in this revolver," I said, "then you decide your next move."

He looked at his gun for a moment, then he turned his head towards me. He squinted his eyes focusing on my gun, then his eyes widen and he slowly pulled his hand away from his own gun.

"How?" he asked.

"I'll show you sometime," I said.

The Lieutenant walked up and kicked the gun away even further from Joseph, he brought his own weapon up and pointed it at Joseph's head.

"You mind cuffing him to a banister," he said, holding out his handcuffs to me.

I holstered my weapon, took the handcuffs, and dragged Joseph over to the railing support post and handcuffed his arms around it.

"Hey, I'm bleeding here, you son's of bitches, you shot me in the ass."

"I'm bleeding too," said the Lieutenant, "so quit you belly aching. Watcher collect their weapons, would you, I need to sit down. While I collected the weapons Lieutenant Sanders walked back into my room. I stood at the top of the stairs and looked down. The night manager was peeking up from behind the reception desk. I walked back to my room.

"Have Hart wrap your arm up while I call the precinct," I said. "We'll need an ambulance and a bus for these guys."

Uniforms were the first on the scene followed quickly by the men with the ambulance. Joseph was complaining that he wasn't being seen quick enough and when they tended to his wound he complained even more about the snickering. The officers were talking to the Lieutenant and me and Joseph kept yelling he had something to say. Lieutenant Sanders walked over to him.

"Is he okay to travel," he asked.

"No, I'm shot," said Joseph.

The ambulance attendant said his wound was leaking, and someone would need to remove the bullet at the hospital.

"You want to remove the handcuffs, so we can take him?" the attendant asked.

The Lieutenant waved a couple of uniforms over. "Joseph, your name is Joseph, right?"

"Screw you flatfoot," said Joseph.

"Well, you're under arrest for attempted murder of a police officer," said Sanders. "These two officers are going with you in the ambulance."

He turned the two officers. "If he shows any signs of escape or agitation, you shoot him again."

Joseph started to say something, but he looked at the two officers and thought better to remain silent. Lieutenant Sanders took off the handcuffs so Joseph could be freed from the railing, then he handcuffed his hands behind him.

"He won't be very comfortable on the stretcher like that," said one of the attendants.

"He won't hurt anyone either," replied Sanders, "including himself."

The men from the coroner's office showed up as Joseph was being taken away. Lieutenant Sanders pointed at the two dead men in the hall and they went to deal with them. The Coroner came up in the elevator and walked out and came over to me. "Three in less than forty-eight hours, that may be a record," he said.

"One of them may be mine," said Sanders, "Watcher doesn't get all the credit."

I motioned for the Lieutenant to come over and talk to me.

"We need Hart to be somewhere else for now. I tried to send my cab away, but I know he's still down there. Okay if I have him take Hart to the office."

"How do you know he's still here?" asked the

Lieutenant.

"Because I can see him down in the lobby," I replied.

The Lieutenant looked around, everyone seemed busy. He walked to the railing and Max waved. The Lieutenant returned to me shaking his head.

"How is it, that you have been in business such a short time, and you seem to already have an army behind you?"

"My winning personality?"

"What's the problem?" he asked.

"Someone has been one step ahead, knowing my movements. I would rather Hart was not involved officially until we know who is pulling strings."

Sanders nodded. He beckoned Hart to come over.

"There is a cab downstairs, the driver is Max, don't ask. He's in the lobby. Have him take you to the office, see you in, and have him come back here for me," I said

I gave Hart the office key and pushed him on his way. He went downstairs to Max who waved he understood and they left.

"What makes you think, someone won't notice him now?" Sanders asked.

"Too may cops, I don't think anyone really knows what he looks like, and Max could lose a tail in this town faster than anyone I know."

"As soon as the sergeant who is on duty shows up, I'm off to the emergency, the ambulance driver waiting for me is about to have apoplexy."

No sooner had he uttered the comment, Sergeant Simon came bounding up the stairs announcing his presence. He spotted me first and started in with accusations until Lieutenant Sanders stepped into his line of vision. He stuttered over the rest words and I really didn't hear or understand what he was saying.

"Simon, why are you here?" asked Lieutenant Sanders, "this is not your shift."

"I heard the call," he said, "and figured you would need my help."

"Try not to be an ass," Sanders said. "Mr. Watcher, may have very well saved my life in this little encounter, so I would take it as a personal favor if you would take his statement and try not to piss him off. I am off to the hospital to get this arm looked after, and I would very much like to see Mr. Watcher arrive there for me to talk to before I go home. Do you think you could manage that for me."

"Uh, sure, Lieutenant," Simon said.

I wish I could report that after Lieutenant Sanders left that my interview with Simon was one of mutual respect, but it is difficult to have any, where there was none. On the positive side, I didn't add another body for the bus to take to the morgue.

I gave Simon the relevant facts excluding the

existence of Richard Hart, or the fact that the two dead mokes had been following me earlier. I identified Joseph as Mrs Stanton's chauffeur. Since I didn't know the other two, I could honestly swear I had not seen them before tonight. Simon suspected that I was holding something back, but I looked down at the clock in the lobby, and innocently asked how long the Lieutenant might be at the hospital.

"Yeah, yeah, get the hell outa here," said Simon. "But don't leave town."

"Where am I going to go?" I asked. "This is the only home I got."

I smiled and headed down the stairs. Max was by the door in the lobby. As I approached he handed me my office keys.

"Your boy is in the inner office, tucked in for the night. No one was interested in our movements when we left here, and no one paid attention when we went up," said Max.

"Thanks, Max. Can you take me to the hospital, and then back to my office."

"I'm gonna make a week's pay off of you in one night. I'll take you anywhere you want to go."

We left the lobby and climbed into Max's cab. The ride to the hospital was uneventful, which should have told me that the Fickle Bitch wasn't done with me just yet. I left Max waiting outside. He settled down in the front seat to nap while I checked in on Lieutenant Sanders.

Did I Mention, Fates Are Fickle Bitches

The nurse at reception was quite nice and said I could go back to emergency. The Lieutenant was being patched up there and he left instructions for me to come on back. His wife and daughter were already there with him.

I got a sudden cold chill, meeting his family was not high on my list of things to do tonight, but it looked like I was not being given any option in the matter. I had no idea how they would react. In a way, I'm why the Lieutenant was here in the first place.

The nurse at the emergency desk looked like all kinds of business and stared at me.

"Look, I am not family, but I was just in a shootout with Lieutenant Sanders," I said. "I understand he is being patched up here."

"You shot him?" she asked.

"No, we were on the same side, I put down the crud that shot him."

Suddenly the all business nurse was all smiles, "201, bed A," she said.

I walked down the hall shaking my head. That was just plain weird. I stepped into the semi-private room where the Lieutenant was sitting on a bed of sorts. His wound had been attended to and he sort of had his shirt on. He looked like he was getting ready to leave.

"Hey Lieutenant, how are you doing?" I stopped dead in my tracks.

"Hi, Watcher," he said, "Come in and meet my wife and daughter."

There stood my new receptionist, Betty her daughter, the waitress, next to his bed. I couldn't really tell from everyone's expressions what was coming down, but I figured it was a good thing I was in an emergency room.

I took a step back and just stared. I did mention that Fate was a Fickle Bitch, right.

Suddenly everyone started talking and I whistled. A Nurse stuck her head in and told us to quiet it down. She suggested we go to the hospital cafeteria and finish our conversation. Talk about taking a long silent walk.

We sat down at a small square table, each with a cup of coffee we weren't drinking. I didn't know if the coffee was that bad or the situation was. I decided to break the ice without really saying anything.

"Will someone say something," I said.

"Thank you," said Betty.

"For..." I started hoping someone would finish.

"For keeping my flatfoot husband from getting his head shot off," she said.

"Hey, wait a minute," interjected the Lieutenant, "he was the one who called me to be there."

"And you couldn't send someone else?" Her look was one of a conversation that had been had before.

"Whoa," I interrupted. "He is right, I did call for him, there wasn't anyone else I could trust. And I was expecting trouble, just not an ambush."

When I said it, wheels started turning in my head, and I made a mental note to get a hold of Max as soon as I could. Clearly it struck a cord with my other companions. The daughter started sipping her coffee with a slight smile on her face.

"What?" I asked.

"Usually I get sent to my room when this conversation starts up," she said.

"Let's deal with the elephant," I said. "When was someone going to tell me that my new receptionist was married to a Lieutenant in Homicide?

"I would like to know without all the family history," I continued.

"She told me the night she came home," Sanders said. "It was a long discussion, but she reminded me that she had been a well-trained police officer and could handle herself in your office. There was a lot more to the conversation, and I am not thrilled with the circumstances..."

"Can you handle a piece?" I asked Betty.

"Hey," said the Lieutenant.

"Yes I can," stepped up Betty.

"Relax, Lieutenant," I said. "I'm not taking

her out into the field. But I will have Fritz set her up with a gun in the desk, for her own protection."

"Oh," said the Lieutenant.

"Why can't I work in the field?" asked Betty.

"I could be the receptionist," said the daughter.

"No!" we three responded in unison,

She just pouted.

"My being a receptionist for now is just fine," said Betty.

I looked at Lieutenant Sanders, who just shrugged. I sighed and in the distant background I could hear the laughter of that Fickle Bitch.

"Remember, to meet me at nine tomorrow morning at Fritz's, the gunsmith south of Market," I said to Betty.

Lieutenant Sanders started to say something, but Betty shot him a look that just brought a sigh. I knew this wasn't over, but just the end of round one. I wanted to get to the office to check on Hart. We said our good-byes.

"And you're welcome," I said to Betty.

She looked at me quizzically

"For him," I answered

She just smiled. The battle was over for the night.

As I left the hospital Max was still parked where I left him, slumped down in the driver's seat fast asleep. I knocked lightly on the driver's side window as I walked around to the passenger's side of the Cab and climbed in. Traffic was light this late and it was easy to determine we weren't being followed from the hospital. There had been enough action for one night, and whoever was behind all this needed to regroup I hoped.

Honestly, Who Gives A Lady A Gun

When we got back to my office I got out of the cab with my coat opened. Just being cautious. I sent Max home and told him to get back to his usual schedule. I'd call if I needed a cab. I paid him and he waved as he left. I was spending Mrs Stanton's money like it was going to be an ongoing income, and while it was sufficient to see me through the rest of the year, I was going to need to adjust my expenses. When I wrapped this case up, the well was going to dry up.

I took the stairs up to my office and knocked on the door when I got there.

"Who, who is it?" asked Hart.

"Relax, kid, it's Watcher," I said.

He slowly opened the door, and looked at me and for the minions in his mind that were ready to rush in on him. I pushed on the door and closed it behind me. I shoved a chair up under the doorknob bracing it.

"Oh," he said, " I never thought of doing that."

"You'll learn," I said, "if you stay in this business. Let's go to the inner office, I want to talk a little more about forensic accounting, and this time you 're going to tell me everything I need to know."

I sat at my desk and Hart in one of the client

chairs. I left the door open and the lights in the outer office off. This gave me a view of the outer door, so if anyone came calling this late I would be ready for them. I didn't really expect anyone, but as an MP I had learned that if you were ready and no one came that was a lot better than not being ready when someone came crashing through your door.

I really wasn't interested in the accounting aspects of the case, but somewhere in Hart's head was the missing piece of the puzzle and I needed it. I didn't let him ramble, I just asked pointed questions and made sure he answered, in short, concise sentences. He complained he was being interrogated, and I told him it was going to be me or SFPD. He agreed he would rather it was me.

It wasn't just Mr. Stanton he had gathered information on, he was also directed to get information on Mrs Stanton. It confused him, because mostly she was an open book, accounting wise.

There were some rather high payments to a private boy's school back east, but she had nephews in the school and she foot the bill for her sister. He commented he thought the sister was taking advantage of her because the numbers didn't add up. The sister had two boys in school, but the money would have supported three. He figured the sister was skimming somehow.

The real story seemed to relate to Mr. Stanton. He had been working for his father when he skipped the first time, to be an artist. That is when Hart thought he was going to skip the country. He had been in Miami and was ready to jump to South America when something happened, he started selling paintings. Not just a few and not for just a couple of bucks. A gallery in Miami was bringing in several grand a week. My missing piece.

I told Hart to take the sofa in the inner office, and I would take the one in reception, I wanted to go over the report and the notes he made. I had a funny feeling that Stanton had done something stupid, and it bit him in the ass because it turned out he didn't have to in the first place. I needed to talk to someone back east with National, someone high up who knew Stanton's father, maybe Stanton's father himself.

It was about two in the morning when I drifted off with a bit of a self-satisfied smug feeling. I had most of it figured out. Now I had to prove it and keep from becoming one of the dearly departed before I could lay it all out for the police.

In the morning, I made coffee and woke up Hart. It was about eight o'clock and I needed to meet Betty at Fritz's before I met with the Lieutenant back here at the office. While we had coffee I layed out my basic plans for Hart. He had a dazed look as he followed my monologue.

"Okay," I said, "do you have someplace you can go to out of the city?"

"Friends in the east bay," he replied. "I can

114

take the ferry over and have them pick me up."

"Good, you do that, call the office when you get there and let my receptionist know you are safe and sound, and then I will put the rest of my plan into action. I don't want you near where you can get hurt."

I called Max and had him pick up Hart, then I left for Fritz's.

Betty was inside when I got there. She was looking around at the different weapons. Fritz came from behind the curtain with a look of disdain.

"She says, she's with you," he said.

"She is," I replied. "She needs a weapon for the office. I want a setup in the desk behind the modesty panel so she can have quick access in case she needs to deal with a critical situation."

"You know my rules, she has to be able to break it down, clean it and shoot. Is okay Miss?" he said to Betty.

She nodded, "It's missus."

"Close me up, Jonas and let's see what the lady can do," said Fritz motioning Betty to enter the back of the shop. "You want a twenty-two?"

"I would prefer a thirty-eight," she said.

"A serious gun," said Fritz.

We walked into the back room and Fritz had Betty sit at one of the work areas. He grabbed a gun from the shelf and laid it down before Betty.

"Take it apart, clean it, put it back together,

115

you show me."

Betty checked that the revolver was empty and then expertly broke it down placing the pieces on the bench before her. She wiped them down, applied oil, wiped them down again. She checked the barrel and cleaned it. Then she reassembled the gun.

"Nice," said Fritz, "I would have placed the bits differently, but I pick a nit there. Let us go down to the range and see if you can shoot."

Down in the range, Fritz gave Betty six bullets. She loaded and waited for his signal to fire. Betty took aim and fired all six shots. Even from the distance we were at I could see Fritz was impressed with her skill level. He had Betty reel in her target and we went back up to the back room.

"You could shoot like this before you were married," he asked.

"I could," Betty replied.

"And your husband knew this about you?"

"Yes, he did."

"He must love you very much, and I am sure he is very faithful," said Fritz. Then he laughed.

"I will have a holster to put under the desktop for you later today at your office. I will keep the gun and bring it with me," said Fritz.

"Can I come back to shoot some of the other weapons you have?" she asked.

"If you pay for the ammunition, clean up afterward, you may test any weapon I have that fires," he said.

The walk back to the office was uneventful. We went up in the elevator, exited on the fourth floor and opened up the office, just like any normal business day. Hart had left a note on Betty's desk. It included the address and a phone number where he would be in the East Bay.

"I have one witness safe and sound, now I need to secure the other one," I said. "Betty hold down the fort while I am away. Fritz should be by pretty soon to set up your desk."

"If you get any calls?" she asked.

"Take a message, unless your husband needs to get a hold of me, I'll be at The Palace with Mrs Stanton," I replied.

The Palace: Act III

As I entered the lobby of The Palace, I headed for the barber shop and the shoe shine station to find Billie Whitehall. I knew Mrs Stanton was expecting me, but there were still holes in my theory as to what all was going on. There were two missing players, and they had to be here in San Francisco somewhere for all of this to make sense. I wanted to talk to Billie about who was around before last night. Mrs Stanton had to be under surveillance by someone.

The problem with a lot of operatives doing surveillance is they work at not being seen by the people they're watching, but forget about someone else who might see them. Billie was a very observant man, and my guess is he might have seen who was watching Mrs Stanton.

When I arrived at the shoe shine station, Billie was finishing up with a customer. I waited and climbed into a chair. Billie looked up at me and laughed.

"You are going to wear out you shoes just getting them shined," he said.

"Just buff and talk to me," I said. "I need information, my usual rates."

"I'll slap leather with a rag, you ask your questions and I'll see if I got answers."

"Before last night, did Mrs Stanton meet with anyone, or was anyone watching her?"

Billie whistled while he buffed my shoes, then he slowed down and thought for a moment.

"When she arrived there was a three piece with her carrying a briefcase, smelled like a mouthpiece, expensive too. He was reassuring her about something, but she wasn't having any. Something had her upset.

"Shadows, a man in the shadows, never really got a good look at him. He hung to the shadows. Until last night, if Mrs Stanton was down here, so was he. Her first, though, always. But he wasn't following her, he would usually show up from another direction."

"I wish you could describe him. It's too bad there is no way to identify him," I said.

"Never said I couldn't recognize him," said Billie.

"You said he hung to the shadows and you didn't get a look at him," I reminded him.

"Not him, his shoes. The man wore spats. Who wears spats these days except high society. Another thing, spats met with Joseph last night just before he and the other two took off."

"You didn't mention him last night," I said.

"I didn't know, a maid saw them. In case yo' didn't know it, you now have this place wired, we invisible's are on the job"

I gave Billie a sawbuck and told him to split it with the maid.

"Intend to," he said.

I headed to the elevators and went up to the penthouse floor, apparently I am now known.

The Butler answered the door and admitted me. He showed me to the same alcove I sat in the last time I was here.

"I have kept the apartment on lock-down per your instructions," he said. "The Missus is upset, but she has held up quite well. She is angry and wants to know what is going on. She doesn't like being kept in the dark. Coffee, Sir. She'll be out in a moment."

"Coffee would be great," I said.

He left for the kitchen to get the coffee, and Mrs Stanton appeared almost as if on cue.

"Would you mind telling me what's going on," she said.

"You lied to me, Mrs Stanton," I said very matter of factually.

"I, what!" she said indignantly.

"You knew your husband was dead and you hired me to find him," I said. "Did you want me to find his body, confirm he was dead or find his killer. It would have been helpful to know from the start that he was already dead. Or maybe you killed him and needed to know if you got away with it."

I spoke sharply and pushed hard. She started shaking her head. She cried she didn't know. She insisted she just wanted to know where he was. She just wanted to know what had happened to him.

"When he died!" I said harshly.

"Yes!" she snapped back.

I sat back in my chair and just stared at her.

The butler entered with a tray. "Coffee, Sir?" he asked.

He set down the tray on the table between Mrs Stanton and me. He poured both cups of coffee and served them. Mrs Stanton looked to him for support, but he performed his routine as the perfect butler and returned to the kitchen. She watched him go, her eyes widened when he closed the kitchen door.

"Will no one help me," she said.

"If you start telling me the truth," I said, "I will."

"I didn't know he was dead," she said. "I suspected he was. Things didn't seem quite right after New Orleans."

"Did he get the money back to his Father?" I asked.

Her eyes got even wider, she looked really scared. She twisted around looking for specters, or a place to run.

"Relax, Mrs Stanton," I said. "No one else knows about his embezzling from his Father's associates. Not even the ones who killed him."

"He didn't embezzle, he stole. How did you know?" she asked.

"Forensic accounting," I said. "Not me, a National employee found it out, but even he

121

doesn't really know it, what happened. You want to start from the beginning. Before Miami."

Suddenly Mrs Stanton relaxed, I half expected her to collapse from the release of the stress, then she straightened up.

"Martin Stanton was a pig," she said. "How far back do I go?"

"Start with the truth about the first time he left," I said

"He had been working for his father, and he was bored. That's when he got less than discrete about his liaisons. I thought he was simply going to ask for a divorce. That would have been fine with me.

"But all of a sudden he got real secretive. He said he was headed out of town. He took a brief trip to Miami. When he came back, things seemed to get back to normal. Then he took another trip. At the time, I didn't know where. Then he was dealing with someone in Miami a lot. He set up a studio there. He always liked to paint. His first dalliances were models. The funny thing was he seemed to be a pretty good artist. Anyway, he set up in Miami and would take trips to paint. Everyone, me included assumed he was meeting with a model he was keeping down there."

"Okay, that's the setup," I said. "How did he break the news that he wasn't coming back?"

"Actually he threatened me. He said he was going to leave the country, he had done something, and he needed three more months but he couldn't keep making trips back and forth, so I was going to have to help him. If I didn't..."

"I know about your son, Mrs Stanton," I said.

"No one knows..."

"Well, I do. I was looking for a reason you would co-operate with your husband. Love for someone else was the only thing that would persuade you to help him. You didn't care about scandal, if you did you would have never married him in the first place. Of course, you did care about scandal when you were a lot younger. You wouldn't have hidden your son from your family and the world otherwise."

"You don't know my father," she said.

"No, I don't," I replied, "but the boy is what six, seven. When this is over, and it is about to be, go home. Get your son and introduce him to your father. If the kid's last name isn't Parks, change it, trust me. So just what did Martin do, and what did you do for him?" I asked.

"He robbed a bank in upstate New York." she said.

"What in a small Podunk town," I laughed. "What did he get, two three grand?"

"A quarter of a million dollars," she said.

You could have knocked me over with a feather. We're barely recovering from the depression and he scores a quarter of a million dollars. Then it all came together; his father, his father's business associates, National, it all made very scary sense to me.

"He robbed a 'bank', not just some city trust and fund, he hit a mob bank! Holy Shit! And You knew!" I said.

"Not at first. I knew it was bad, but I didn't know the extent of it until I took the trip down to Miami. The men whose bank he hit, didn't know it was him. He hit it at night. No one even knew he knew that the bank was mobbed up. He was working late one night for his father, it was chance that he saw a piece of paper that hadn't been destroyed. Anyway, he became obsessed with it. He spent months working it out. He quit working for his father. They fought about he wanting to be an artist.

"His father always threatened to cut him off. He planned it all. The big problem was moving the money from where he had it stashed to Miami. Then he had to come up with a reason to have so much money."

"He needed a way to launder it," I said.

"His initial plan was to make it look like he was winning at gambling. He couldn't do that in New York, to close to where he stole the money, and the mob might be looking for something like that."

"Then he realized that they might be looking for some kind of a similar scam in Miami," I said. "So he decided to simply skip the country".

"At first, yes. Then something funny happened. He had put some paintings on display in a gallery in Miami. Five of them sold. Not for too much, several hundred dollars, the asking price," she said.

"Ah, but the birth of an idea," I replied.

"Yes, he would buy the paintings himself, disguised of course. First he jacked up the prices for his paintings. Thousands of dollars. The gallery owner said he was nuts, but since he had some small success, and Martin was willing to pay to have a showing, the gallery owner went along with it.

"The show was a success in that it got a lot of press, and Martin had a couple of shills make purchases at the inflated prices. It would take a little time, but Martin now had a way to account for the fortune he was about to have."

"So what happened?"

"At the end of the second month, Martin was to have bought ten of his paintings, about forty thousand dollars worth. Only sixteen sold, for over a hundred thousand dollars. A couple went to bid because several buyers were interested in his work. Several were from Europe and Martin was a sensation in the European art world. Of the ten Martin thought he was going to buy he only got four."

"That means his shills couldn't get the paintings, so they took off with his money," I laughed.

"Martin couldn't do anything about it," she said, "if he went after them, it would expose his whole plan. He was furious, until he realized he got more money then he set out for."

I laughed, and then thought about it. Martin Stanton was in trouble.

"Except that his shills might figure out what he was doing," I said, " Unless they were too scared that Martin might come after them. Martin had to change venue. More importantly, he no longer had to launder money, he was legitimately making a fortune. He had to get the money back to the mob without them knowing it was he who took it in the first place. They would still be looking for the thief, but not as hard, and if Martin could remain anonymous, he would be in the clear."

I looked at Mrs Stanton and wondered, "Why did you go after him?" I asked aloud.

"That's just it, I didn't. He told me what happened in Miami at the gallery, he told me I could have a divorce as long as I didn't want anything from him. He was finally going to be out of my life. I was thrilled to be free of him."

"What went wrong?" I asked.

"Initially, nothing. He still needed to get the Mob's money and get it back to New York. He planned to use his father as a go-between, anonymously of course. He decided to continue to sell paintings in Miami, then New York, and finally Europe. But someone found out about the bank."

"Then why get National involved?" I asked.

"Martin needed to continue the ruse, He had a friend at National, everything was supposed to go through him. Martin had to be on the lam so to speak. I would provide the red herring of his moving and sending him money through National.

"Martin actually went to St Louis. With Martin's friend at National, we could set up a trail to New Orleans. Martin could lay low and paint in St Louis while anyone interested would be looking for him somewhere else. By biding time, Martin could get the mob back its money without anyone finding out he was the guy who robbed the bank and Martin could eventually go live in Europe."

"But you got a surprise from Martin," I said. "He really did go to New Orleans. From there he was supposed to head for South America, only he went to Los Angeles."

"I didn't know what was going on, Martin's contact at National said something had gone amiss, he was trying to track Martin and would let me know as soon as he had an idea as to what was happening."

"Except you got a bad feeling about the man from National and decided to cancel their involvement," I said.

She nodded.

"I suspect he had already been murdered in New Orleans," I said flatly. "Someone was able to tap into what was going on and decided to cut themselves in for a piece of the action. Martin refused to play along, he must have been successful in getting the mob back its money and felt there wasn't any threat to him anymore."

I sat back and thought for a couple of minutes. The immediate threat to Mrs Stanton was no longer active, but I needed to finalize a couple of details.

"You need to pack up and head for the next train back east," I said.

I handed her Max's card.

"Here is the name of a cab to hire, no one else. He'll get you to the train station safely. When you get to Chicago, send me a wire, but you should be in the clear by then. Oh, Joseph will not be accompanying you, he's in jail. When you get to Boston, wire me three grand, our business will be concluded by then. Oh, introduce your father to his grandson."

I got up and said I would show myself out. I shook her hand gently and smiled. She was going to be okay. I hoped the same could be said for me. I had a murderer to catch, and he wasn't going to go gently into the night.

Never Upset An Armed Receptionist

I didn't know how spats fit into all of this, and I figured I needed to have a face to face with him in order to see what his interest was in this case. He seemed to be connected to the group Joseph was with, but they were mostly low-level thugs on an assigned mission, to get the information that Hart had. Spats could be the brains behind it, but I think he would have shown up earlier in the picture if he was a major player. On the other hand, he could be either William Mason, or Sam Parrish, though I doubted it.

William Mason and Sam Parrish both worked for National, and Mason seemed to be Martin's contact in National. He must have been working both sides, he must have been the go-between with Martin, and he must have been skimming when money was involved. He had to be the one altering reports at National for Martin because they had his signature. At some point, he had to have gone into business for himself, or he and Parrish joined forces. Where the hell was Parrish. I know Mason is in San Francisco somewhere, and he seems to be the one running the guys that came at the Lieutenant and me. I needed to get Mason out in the open on my terms, find Parrish, and figure out his involvement. My first move was to see Billy Whitehall, I needed to get a message to Spats and an anonymous delivery at The Palace was my best bet.

Mrs Stanton would be in the Hotel one more night, because she had already missed today's train back east. According to Billie, Spats showed up in the lobby when Mrs Stanton came down from her suite. That meant that Spats had access, I just hoped it hadn't been Joseph, otherwise I wasn't going to get my face to face. Billie was shining shoes, so I went to one of the lobby alcoves and wrote up a brief message for Spats. I put it into an envelope and went to see Billie.

"I need you to keep an eye out for Spats," I said to Billie.

"He's in the Piper right now," said Billie.

I wondered if the Fickle Bitch was watching out for me or out to get me.

"Okay," I said. "Watch for him, and deliver this for me."

I slipped Billie a five and headed for the front lobby exit. I wanted to get back to the office as quickly as possible. I needed to get there before Spats. I needed to alert Betty that we might be getting a guest who might be a little dangerous.

I got a cab pretty quick, but clearly the driver didn't understand what in a hurry meant. He tried a couple of turns that were out of line. It took my informing him, I was packing heat, and he was pissing me off, before he finally got that he should focus on getting me to my destination quickly. The traffic and red lights were not his fault. Still when we got to my office I tossed him his fare sans tip.

I went up in the elevator and out of habit I opened my coat. I had a sudden bad feeling and when the doors opened I looked in both directions before exiting the elevator. I walked to the office. I put my hand on the door and opened it slowly. I could see Betty, and she was not happy. I don't know what happened, but I figured I would find out from the Lieutenant what would be the best way to apologize. I stepped into the office.

"You expecting company?" she asked.

"Yes," I said hesitantly.

"You couldn't give me a heads up?" she asked.

"I thought I would be here before my guest arrived," I said, " Everything okay?"

"He's in the office. He had to get his own coffee. He called me honey!" she said.

It was then that I saw the snub nose on her desk,

"His?" I asked.

"Yes," She replied. "When he arrived, he seemed agitated. I could see the bump in his coat. He really should get a better tailor. I explained that unknown visitors were required to hand over any armament until they were fully vetted. He was reluctant to give it up. I retrieved the thirty-eight from under the desk and pointed it at his manhood and explained if he didn't comply I would perform a briss upon him. Fritz did an excellent job. I can retrieve the gun quickly in a single motion and

131

display its presence. It's quite effective."

"I'll see, uh Mr...."

"He said his name was Smith," she replied.

"Next time I'll call and give you a heads up," I said.

"You do that," she replied.

Spats, Mr. Smith was sitting in the client chair. He was an older man slightly heavy thinning gray hair. He was wearing a three-piece suit, he might have been a banker or lawyer. He was drinking a cup of coffee, it was clear he hadn't been waiting long. He turned and looked at me.

"You have me at a slight disadvantage," he said. "You're armed, and I am not."

"If you thought you were in any danger," I said, "you would not have come or you would have brought reinforcements. I think I made it clear in my note that I wanted to talk, possibly exchange information that would be mutually illuminating for both of us. And you know who I am, and I don't know who you are. So I don't think you are at a disadvantage at this moment."

"Your receptionist is remarkable, would it be possible to persuade her to come work for me?" he asked.

"She's married, and I don't think she wants to work in New York," I replied.

It was a shot in the dark, but he blinked, and he knew he blinked.

"Well played, Mr. Watcher," he said. "I

would be fascinated to hear how you got mixed up in this."

"Kismet," I replied.

Mr. Smith nodded. "You do still have me at a disadvantage"

"Betty," I called out, "bring Mr. Smith his weapon, I think we have reached an understanding."

Betty walked in casually with Mr. Smith's gun. She handed it to him slowly noting I had my right hand on my gun.

"An understanding, huh," she said.

Mr. Smith had to turn away from me to take his gun and Betty was to one side so that Mr. Smith made an excellent target if he tried to grab her. He slowly took his gun with two fingers and gently slipped it into his jacket. Then he buttoned his coat and I removed my right hand from my gun.

Mr. Smith looked up at Betty.

"I apologize for the 'honey' reference," he said, "I underestimated you, I don't do that very often, it won't happen again."

Betty nodded and went back to her desk leaving the door ajar. Mr. Smith turned back to me.

"Since you showed faith in returning my gun to me, I will answer what questions I can," he said.

"Have you been in San Francisco long?" I

asked.

He cocked his head and looked at me.

"An odd question," he said, "I have been here a couple of days. I arrived in the city by train before you took up residence in this office. You were a surprise. My employers know very little about you."

"I think, maybe you will be more forthcoming if I provide you some information you may not know," I said. "Martin Stanton is dead. He died in New Orleans."

Mr. Smiths eyes widened, then his gaze narrowed as he gauged if the information I just gave him was true or not.

"You have proof of this," he said rather than asked.

"No direct proof, mostly circumstantial. But I can give you sufficient information, so that any contacts you have in New Orleans can confirm what I say is true. Also, your employers have recently received something that was taken from them in upstate New York, would you like details."

"I have been informed that a wire is waiting for me back at my hotel, I suspect that it will most likely confirm what you just said. Why?" he asked.

"Martin Stanton took what was not his because he wanted to get away from his father. The irony is that his artistic ability provided a much larger watershed than his theft. He attempted to make amends anonymously and head for Europe sans wife. Someone ended his dream before he could make it a reality."

Mr. Smith leaned back in his chair brought his hands together, interlaced his fingers upon his chest and tucked his chin down as he stared at my desk. He sat for a couple of minutes thinking.

"You deduced most of this?" he asked.

"I have," I replied.

"What do you want?"

"Nothing from you, except leave Mrs Stanton alone. She was not part of the theft, in fact, her primary activity was to assist your employers getting their money back. Any other involvement was coerced"

"Convince me?"

"She has a son, not Martin's. He threatened the boy."

"If I can confirm what you have told me, I have no interest in the wife. But Martin Stanton had a partner. My employers are concerned about how they were robbed. My job..."

I smiled. While Mr. Smith was a most dangerous man, I realized he was not a problem.

"You're in domestic service," I said.

He sat upright in his chair, and I might have been concerned, but I knew he didn't get the joke.

"You clean up after people," I said.

Mr. Smiths eyes softened and then he laughed, "My God, Mr. Watcher, I do like you.

Domestic Service, I think I will put that on a business card."

"There are three people in this case that might be connected with Martin Stanton. All three are or were employees of National; William Mason, Sam Parrish, and Steven Jaxom. Jaxom came too late to be Martin's partner, but Mason or Parrish were in the frame from close to the beginning. Mrs Stanton said Martin had a friend at National who was doctoring the reports so Martin could make good on his getaway."

Mr. Smith nodded, "Jaxom is an opportunist who might take advantage of a situation as long as it doesn't get too messy. Mason is not in San Francisco. As for Stupid Sammy..."

"Stupid Sammy," I said.

"Mason called him something like that, anyway, I have no idea where he's at," said Mr. Smith as he stood up. "I'll see myself out. I will be in touch, I don't really have any information for you."

"Oh, but you did," I said.

"What is that?" he asked.

"If I kill anyone else involved in this, your employers don't care, as long as they get the information they want," I said.

"I believe you are correct," he said.

"Mr. Smith, I know you are also a point man. Please convey to your employers, San Francisco is really too small to invest in for expansion. It really would be too expensive."

Again Mr. Smith eyed me carefully, "You have only been working out of this office a couple of days, being a little aggressive, aren't you?"

I slowly stood up and faced him. "I found you in that time," I said.

Mr. Smith laughed again, "I do like you Mr. Watcher. I agree. For other reasons as well, San Francisco is not worth cultivating for my employers. We will talk again before I leave."

Mr. Smith nodded and went out of my office. He said good-bye to Betty and was gone. I took a deep breath. Mr. Smith told me a lot more than he realized.

Betty entered my office and stood in the doorway.

"Just who was he?" she asked.

"He works for Martin Stanton's Father's business associates. He provides a number of services that involves cleaning. He was genuinely surprised that Martin Stanton is dead. He is not yet convinced of his demise. He is not a part of this case. He was, however, most informative by his lack of knowledge. He was following Mrs Stanton, believing she was Martin's contact. Now that he has information that she is not, he will follow that up. Which is to our benefit."

"How?" she asked.

"He has resources at his disposal, that I do not. I was forthcoming with him to a point, and I expect he will discover the gaps in what I have told him. He will confirm what I suspect and then he will contact me."

"Can you trust him?" she asked.

"Oh yes, if he tells you he is going to kill you he most certainly will."

Just then the outer door opened, Betty turned quickly, and judging by the instant change in her demeanor, I knew it was the Lieutenant who had just come in.

"Please Lieutenant," I said, "come in."

He appeared at my office door. "how the hell did you know.."

I pointed at Betty. "She doesn't look like that when I come in here," I said.

"Betty," I said, "lock the outer door, and then come on back in, we'll catch up."

Lieutenant Sanders sat on the sofa and we waited for Betty to return. She sat down in one of the client chairs.

"I passed a man in the lobby, packing heat, was he a visitor here," Lieutenant Sanders asked.

"Was he wearing spats?" I asked.

Lieutenant Sanders nodded.

"He was," I said. "Your wife smoothly disarmed him."

"She disarmed him," he said.

"He had a small caliber snub nose, and I had a thirty-eight," she said, "it was simply a matter of superior fire power."

"And his desire to keep his manhood intact," I said.

Lieutenant Sanders closed his eyes and shook his head. Then he looked at Betty, "You're enjoying this."

"Shouldn't I," she asked innocently.

"Jeez, Betty." Then he looked at me. "Is he involved with Mickey's death?"

"His interests run in a parallel investigation with some overlap, but he is not directly involved with what happened to Mickey Philips," I said. "Though he may be able to provide us with some information that could lead to Mickey's killer."

Lieutenant Sanders nodded and leaned back and in his chair.

"I received some interesting news this morning from a friend back east in Washington."

He turned to Betty, "I have some background on your new boss. I think you should hear it."

I already had a pretty good idea about what the Lieutenant was going to spill, and I thought he was being a little melodramatic. I really wasn't interested in hearing my background discussed, but it was something I was going to have to sit through.

"Colonel Thompson was very interested in learning where you were. He's a little pissed with you. You wouldn't re-up."

"Eight years was enough," I said.

"Jonas Watcher was among the last of the ten thousand who were shipped to Europe at the end of the war," he said to Betty. "He received a field promotion to officer which was sustained. For the last six years of service in Europe, he served under the Provost Marshal in the military police as a criminal investigator. Your boss was a Captain in the Military Police."

He turned to me and stared hard. "What the hell happened?"

"A whole lot more than I want to cover here," I said. "Let's just say that peace time in the good ol' US of A was not what I expected."

"You became a drunk," he said.

"Yeah," I replied, "and I am still on the edge, so can we just get to the business at hand."

"There isn't much more. William Mason is still in the wind, Joseph is in jail, and apparently Sam Parrish has fallen off the face of the earth. We are no closer to Mickey's killer," Lieutenant Sanders said.

"I believe that one of the three men from National killed Mickey," I said. This whole case is about a lot of money, close to a half million dollars, maybe more. I don't have a number of how many paintings Martin Stanton sold, or for how much. But between liquidating and moving and investing money, Hart's notes indicate that is the fortune that Martin accumulated."

Lieutenant Sanders whistled.

"Who's got it?" he asked.

"Whoever is pulling strings," I said. "Look, let's wrap this up for the night. I need to get my head around this some more, maybe something will materialize by morning."

We said our good-byes and all left the office together. I headed to my apartment, and the Sanders headed for home. I didn't hear the Fickle Bitch laughing in the background, maybe she was losing interest.

The Palace: Reprise

When I got to the office the next morning, Betty had already arrived and there was freshly brewed coffee on the hotplate. It smelled good. I poured myself a cup of coffee and sat down in the cushy chair behind my desk? I opened the Stanton file trying to figure out if I missed anything else.

After awhile the outer office door swung open and in flew Lieutenant Sanders. He passed Betty without so much as a hello and stormed into my office.

"Joseph made bail! I don't know how he even got before a judge. I have a couple of boys on him for now. I also sent Simon to take care of Mrs Stanton until she can get on the train later today."

"Who signed the paperwork?" I asked.

Lieutenant Sanders just looked at me. "I'll call the courthouse."

He started to pick up the phone, when Betty yelled from her desk, she was already on it.

"Jeez," said Lieutenant Sanders, "I don't get this kind of response at work."

After a few moments, Betty came in with her notepad.

"It's because I don't work there anymore. The processing officer was Sergeant Simon Church," she said.

"Simple Simon," shouted Lieutenant Sanders"

"Not Stupid Sammy," I said, "Simple Simon, how long has Simon been with the SFPD?"

"About a month, I guess. He was with the New York Police Department, he's been fully vetted," replied Lieutenant Sanders.

"Betty, get Hart on the line for me," I said.

She hurried to her desk and made a call.

"What if Parrish was Martin's inside man? I asked.

"Got him," yelled Betty.

"Ask him Parrish's full name," I said.

"You think Parrish and Church are the same man?" Lieutenant Sanders asked.

"Parrish falsified reports for Martin Stanton at National. I'm sure he was quite capable of forging documents about being a cop, and he probably has enough buddies to back him up."

"Sam, no, it's Simon," called Betty.

"We have to get to The Palace and now!" I said.

"Look, Watcher, what else do you have other than a reference of a first name?" he asked.

"Who okay-ed the paperwork for Joseph to see a judge? And where was Simon when Mickey got shot? How was it he showed up at my place after the shoot out, it wasn't his shift?"

The Lieutenant called the precinct and spoke with the desk sergeant. He asked about the order and then "uh huh" a lot before hanging up the phone.

"When Simon signed the order, he told the desk sergeant I wanted Joseph out on the street to be tailed. When I ordered the tail this morning after Joseph had been released, the desk sergeant didn't give it another thought. We'll take my car," he said. "make sure you have refills for that hog leg of yours."

I patted my pocket, got up and we left.

When we climbed in the car, Lieutenant Sanders got on the radio and called in to the precinct as he started the engine and pulled into traffic with lights and siren.

"I need the status of Sergeant Church," he said.

"Checked out for the day," said the voice over the radio. "Said he was on an undercover case at The Palace and we should stay away as not to break his cover."

"Well his cover is blown, he is about to become a kidnapper, and I don't know what else. Where is Joseph?"

"We pulled his tail per Sergeant Church," said the voice on the radio.

"Jeez, send patrol cars to The Palace and cordon off the streets, Sergeant Church is a person of interest in a potential kidnapping, he is not, repeat, not to be allowed to leave the area. If possible take him into custody."

Lieutenant Sanders dropped the radio mike and shouted out more expletives in a shorter amount time than I have ever heard anyone do.

While lights and siren are nice, drivers still don't know what to do when you are coming up on them. The good news was they were already setting up barricades when we arrived at The Palace. The bad news was we had no idea where Simon was or what his plan was.

We pulled up along side of one of the police cruisers and got out. Lieutenant Sanders spoke with the police officer in charge.

"There are two men, Joseph Pestori, Mrs Stanton's chauffeur, and Sergeant Church. I suspect their plan is to kidnap Mrs Stanton, but for the life of me I don't know why," he said to the officer.

"It's because they don't know where the accumulated money is," I said.

"And Mrs Stanton does," said Lieutenant Sanders.

"No, she has no idea," I replied, "These two along with William Mason have been chasing this since Martin Stanton left Miami."

"Then there's three of them," said the patrol officer.

"No," I said, "Mason's dead. He's must be one of the bodies in the morgue, I don't know which one. Run their photo's passed National, I'm pretty sure one of them is a match. Remember, except for Mickey no one has ever seen Mason, not even Hart."

"What!" interjected Lieutenant Sanders. "I thought he was the brains… Was he hired help or a partner?"

"Partner," I said, "but not the brains."

"Let's deal with these two, then you can fill me in later," said Lieutenant Sanders.

We headed for The Palace lobby. Our hope was that we got there before Simon and Joseph with Mrs Stanton. As soon as we walked through the front doors, Billie Whitehall waved to us. I pointed him out to Lieutenant Sanders and we went over to see him.

"I saw Mrs Stanton's chauffeur and one of the detectives go up in the elevator just a while ago," he said. "The detective pulled his badge at the front desk to get access to the penthouse. He said something about Mrs Stanton being under investigation. He was being a bully about it which didn't make sense to me. Also, what is the chauffeur doing out of jail?"

"Long story short, they're kidnapping Mrs Stanton," I said.

"Is there a service elevator to the penthouse floor?" asked Lieutenant Sanders.

"Yep, it opens off the hall to the back and the kitchen," said Billie.

"That's where they'll go to take her out. They won't risk trying to take her out the front," said Lieutenant Sanders.

"Billie, get everyone away from that hall. There are about to be some fireworks," I said.

Billie pointed the way to the hall and we started running, I pulled my colt and cocked it. I carried it wide and pointed down. Lieutenant Sanders pulled his automatic and held it barrel up. Billie started pulling various workers aside and pointed them in the opposite direction.

There were double swinging doors with portholes into the back hall. We paused long enough to determine that there wasn't anyone waiting for us. Billie broke into the kitchen to keep the staff from using the hall. There was a corner for us to turn before we would get eyes on the elevator.

We paused waited and listened. I took a quick look. The hall was empty and the back doors to the outside on the opposite wall were closed. The familiar bell of an arriving elevator sounded. I ducked my head back and indicated we go on three. We could hear footsteps and we knew that they would head in the opposite direction towards the back doors.

"Screw three," said Lieutenant Sanders. "Now!"

We each moved to an opposite wall of the hall and the Lieutenant shouted for Simon and Joseph to stop. Neither had a gun displayed. Simon swung around and pulled Mrs Stanton to in front of him. He wasn't a particularly tall man so she was pretty good cover for him.

Joseph was left out in the open with no cover so he did the only thing a stupid man would do he pulled his gun and swung around, I didn't give him time to pick a target, I shot him in the shoulder, that swung him back against a wall. His hand with the gun hit the wall with enough force to knock the gun to the floor.

Simon took the opportunity to pull a gun, and I cocked mine, both Lieutenant Sanders and I had a bead on Simon. Joseph slid to the floor complaining he had been shot again. He was too far from his gun to be a threat any longer. Simon was standing straight ahead of me and Lieutenant Sanders had him at an angle.

"There is no place for you to go, Church, or should I call you Parrish." said Lieutenant Sanders.

"Well aren't you the clever one, or is it your shamus friend here who figured it out."

Simon pointed his gun at Mrs Stanton's head.

"Drop your, guns, or the little lady dies," he threatened.

"Don't be an idiot, Simon," said Lieutenant Sanders, "She's the only thing keeping you alive."

"Nice try, Lieutenant," he said with a sneer, "but I've been working with you. All you would do is watch her die."

"Not, me," I said, "I'm tempted to put a bullet through her into you, just to take you down."

"Hold on," said Lieutenant Sanders.

"You made a serious mistake, in not letting Mrs Stanton change shoes, Simon. A woman in heels can't run very fast, all she can do is step down hard."

I had raised my voice when I said Mrs Stanton, and when she looked at me, she knew I was talking to her. She had used her heel last night to deal with a drunk. She was already ahead of me when I said "heel", she raised her foot and she brought the spike down hard on his foot and then she dropped as dead weight. Simon yelled, and when he went to recover his grip on her, he was already exposed. Lieutenant Sanders automatic cracked the silence twice and Simon took two in the chest, he tried aiming his gun and as his hand wavered so I took aim at it and pulled the trigger. The gun went flying harmlessly onto the floor.

Mrs Stanton broke free and ran to me. I took her in my arms and cradled her. Lieutenant Sanders walked up to Simon as he slid to the floor. Joseph started for his gun, and I cocked mine again. Joseph looked up and stopped. Lieutenant Sanders stood above Simon.

"That's for Mickey, you son of a bitch."

Simon expelled his last breath.

Lieutenant Sanders yelled, "Clear." The back door swung open and a small contingent of cops raced through the doors. Lieutenant Sanders pointed to Joseph and told them to take him to the hospital and not to let him out of their sights. He told another cop to get the bus for Simon. He holstered his weapon and I did the same with mine.

I turned with Mrs Stanton and walked her out into the lobby. Billie Whitehall was out there and he handed Mrs Stanton a glass of water. He looked at me and shrugged. She took the water and smiled at him. We walked to the elevator and I took her back to her room.

Intermission

It was late afternoon when I returned to the Discrete Inquiries office. I told Betty to take off the rest of the day. She set up the coffee for me, and there were sandwiches from the diner, all I had to do was turn on the hot plate to start up the coffee. I watched the water boil up into the upper bowl and then the coffee drip down while I ate half a sandwich.

I took off the upper bowl of the pot and put it into the bathroom sink. I poured myself a cup of coffee. I went over to my desk and sat down. There was a message on my desk.

"Mr. Smith called," it said.

There was a number to call back. I sighed and took out my gun. I opened it up and pulled the cylinder. I removed the spent cartridges and replaced them with new ones. I reloaded the cylinder, re-holstered the colt, and finished the second half of the sandwich I was eating.

I picked up the phone and called the number Hart had given me. It was a brief conversation, he was in the clear.

There was a knock at the door and then the familiar voice of Lieutenant Sanders.

"Watcher, you home, don't shoot, it's just me." he said.

"Come on in, pour yourself a cup of coffee," I

replied. "There's a sandwich here if you want it."

He slowly walked in, saw the mostly full pot and poured himself a cup and grabbed the sandwich. He walked over to a client chair, sat down, and put his feet up on my desk. He sipped at the coffee and ate the sandwich.

"Betty makes a good pot of coffee," he said.

"Are you okay with her here?" I asked.

"Are you kidding, last night... Never mind, yeah I'm okay with it."

We both took sips from our cups.

"This isn't over yet, is it." he said rather than asked.

"It is for you," I said. "There are aspects of this case that affect people who live on the other side of the country."

"And you?" he asked.

"Yeah, and me. I think I ended up being the wild card that messed everything up for the crew that was going to cut out with close to half a million dollars. Only one man was going to eventually get away with the money.

"His plan was to take out his partners one at a time. Perfume Eddy was to take care of Mason, only he was incompetent. I think Simon got word to Mason, that he was a target. Mason then laid low until Simon let him know about Hart. The odd thing was, Hart was a red herring. None of his information would lead to the money.

"Whoever was in this with Martin had hoped

that Simon, Joseph, and Mason would get into a battle with each other. He would only have to worry about who was left and he would be the last man standing. I think it was Joseph who tried to drown me. I suspect the running bag was supposed to provide enough evidence on Joseph killing me to take him out of the picture, but I survived and got tossed into the mix and it all went awry. It's funny, the plan worked anyway."

"Well you were right, Mason was one of the men who bushwhacked us in your hotel. The other guy was a cousin, of all people, Eddy," said Lieutenant Sanders.

"That just left Simon and Joseph," I said, "All he had to do was misinform them that Mrs Stanton knew where the money was. Then wait for the police to take care of his remaining partners."

"You know who he is?" Lieutenant Sanders asked.

"I'm pretty sure I do," I said. "I'm hoping Mr. Smith will deliver him, or rather I'll deliver him for Mr. Smith."

"What does that mean," he asked.

"It means that you go home to your wife, it's over for you, these are out of towners and it is their personal business. We let them handle it. They will take it away from here. It's a win win for everyone."

Lieutenant Sanders finished his coffee and finally stood up. The phone rang. I waved him away. Slowly and reluctantly he left.

The Dock By The Bay: Reprise

I picked up the phone.

"Hello?"

"Mr. Watcher, this is Mr. Smith," said the voice on the phone.

"You lied to me, Mr. Smith," I said. "Mason was not back east, he was in the city morgue."

"I apologize, Mr. Watcher, But for me Mason was irrelevant. I didn't know where Sam Parrish was. It did not occur to me hc had joined the police force. Plus I still didn't know who Martin's inside partner was."

"Well now we both know, don't we," I said.

"Indeed, but I have no proof. And he does carry a certain amount of weight with my employers," said Mr. Smith.

"You can contact him," I said.

"Yes."

"He doesn't know you suspect him?"

"No, he does not."

"You got witnesses?" I asked.

"I can get them," he said.

"The Docks, where it all started for me. Midnight, you have it all set up, and I will be there."

"Why?" he asked.

"Two reasons," I said. "I want answers, and you will owe me."

"Excellent, I agree. You get to be the sacrificial lamb. What makes you think you can trust me?"

"I can't, but your employers can. And I'm not the sacrificial type, just the bait to bring him out."

I hung up, sat back and finished my coffee.

When it came time to leave the office, I put on the fedora and overcoat. I stopped by Betty's desk to pick up her additional piece of hardware just in case. Mr. Smith had his own agenda to satisfy his employers and my health didn't really matter as long as he came away with the outcome he wanted. He wasn't a direct threat to me, but I'm not sure how much help he would be if I needed defending. On the other hand, Betty's thirty-eight would provide me with some extra support if I needed it.

It was another damp night at the wharf. I climbed on to the dock and moved out of the illumination of the light from the pier above. I was sure Martin's partner wouldn't come alone and while cover was scarce, darkness wasn't. Two men arrived at the pier above and looked around, neither was going to descend the ladder. They both scanned the area carefully, and finally one of them called out.

"Mr, Watcher, I know you are here, I saw you climb down the ladder."

I stayed in the shadows for the moment and listened. I could only hear the movement of the water breaking onto the pylons. I wondered if the

155

two men above me could hear it.

"Did you really believe Mr. Smith would give me up. I have a far greater reach than you know. You should have quit with Sam Parrish. Lieutenant Sanders was satisfied, why weren't you?"

"I take it personally when someone tries to have me killed, Mr. Jaxom," I said.

"Ah, my identity is known to you. I was afraid of that. It wasn't anything personal, Jonas, may I call you Jonas. You were a drunk that Joseph was to kill. We would have seen to it that there would have been plenty of evidence to convict Joseph. Your death would have been avenged. How was I to know that Joseph was an incompetent killer?" said Jaxom.

"Why would he try to kill me, what was to be his motive?" I asked.

"He thought you were a witness."

"He must have had apoplexy when he saw me in the office the next day," I said.

Only he hadn't. Joseph wasn't that good of an actor. It wasn't him on the Pier that night. Jaxom was lying. But why?

"He called me right after, I thought he was going to lose it. I considered taking him out myself, but Mr. Parrish assured me he had it under control."

So someone else had been on the pier that night. Someone else had knocked me into the water. It wasn't Mr Smith, he was too big. Who was Jaxom playing to?

Jaxom's associate moved away putting distance between himself and Jaxom. I figured he was trying to get a bead on my voice. I moved quietly making sure I was on the move when I asked my next question.

"Since Martin had the address to the bank, why did he need you," I asked?

Jaxom turned his head slightly he wasn't sure where my voice had come from. They were about to make their move. I wasn't sure what they had in mind, and Jaxom's associate was now in the darkness as well.

"The address was worthless without the access keys of the bank. I had those," he said. "I had made copies a long time ago. You didn't think Stanton thought it up all on his own did you? I spent months cultivating him. He was to die in Miami, with the money gone."

"But he kept traveling back and forth and painting. Then he wanted to return the money. That must have pissed you off," I said.

"It was my money, Jonas, not his. Then he disappeared. The money was vanishing, then all of a sudden there was so much more. It was mine, you see."

I reached in and pulled out my colt cocking it as I pulled it. I recognized the sound of the flare being lit. I followed that and the sight of the igniting flare. Jaxom's associate held it too long. I fired dead center at it then I dropped and rolled to return to my feet. The flare flew into the air but it was off target. Jaxom swore and had already pulled his gun, an automatic by the looks of it, and he had a bead on me, but the two barks were from a twenty-two, not Jaxom's automatic and he crumpled.

Mr. Smith walked into the light and bent over Jaxom and shot him in the head. He holstered his gun and searched Jaxom. I holstered my gun and climbed the ladder. Mr. Smith found what he was looking for and straightened up. He smiled as I approached him.

"I had lost sight of his assistant," Mr. Smith said, "I am glad you didn't."

"I thought you needed Jaxom alive," I said.

"No, just proof of his duplicity. The items I have taken from him will be more than enough for my employers."

He reached into his side pocket and retrieved an envelope. He handed it to me. I reached out and took it.

"What's this," I asked.

"For your services, please do not refuse it, there are no strings. If anything I am still in your debt." Then he laughed. "Poor Jaxom, he set you up to die. You were supposed to be a worthless derelict. The police would have taken any evidence that Jaxom provided simply to close the case.

"I checked you out, Captain. Even my employer's counter parts in Europe have respect for you. The one man in San Francisco that Jaxom should have avoided was you."

"Yeah, fate is a Fickle Bitch," I said.

"Indeed she is," agreed Mr. Smith.

"I have some colleagues joining me shortly. Do have your Lieutenant stand down. If you will both quickly leave, this will all disappear without a trace. It really isn't of interest to the SFPD."

I looked around and saw Lieutenant Sanders in the distance standing next to a building his gun by his side. I offered my hand to Mr. Smith and he looked at it, then me and then he took it firmly.

"You earned your reputation. I think I will leave San Francisco as purely a tourist destination from now on."

"If you come back, we can shoot some eight ball," I said.

"Excellent."

I headed towards Lieutenant Sanders. He holstered his gun and waited for me to get to him.

"Did you really think I would let you come here alone," he said.

"You were an awful long way away," I said.

"I spotted Mr. Smith?" he said.

"Yeah," I replied.

"He was more interested in the other two than you," he said. "So I figured I would wait to see how it played out. We all done now."

"Mostly, there is still the question of who knocked me into the bay," I said.

"Didn't Jaxom say..."

"He lied," I said.

We started walking away from the docks.

"I can't keep calling you Lieutenant," I said, "what's your first name?"

"David," he said.

I stopped and looked at him. He stopped and walked back to me. I held out my hand.

"Hi David, My name is Jonas Watcher, and I'm going to be a Private Investigator in your fair city," I said.

He looked at me and then my hand and back at me, just like Mr. Smith had done. Then he took my hand in a firm non bone crushing grip.

"David, I'm hungry, you want to get something to eat?" I asked

We both started walking, again.

"Pancakes," he suggested.

"Yeah," I replied.

"You're going to be a pain in my ass, aren't you?" he asked.

"Probably," I said

He started looking around as we walked..

"Do you hear women laughing in the distance?" he asked.

I just smiled. Like I said, the Sisters Fate are Fickle Bitches.

The End

The Sisters are Working Overtime...

In New Orleans:

The waitress watched as the two men seated at the window table pretended to eat the daily special. They were more interested in the art gallery across the street than in their meals or conversation with each other. The only time they demonstrated any animated conversation was when they thought someone was watching them. A second waitress approached her and nodded at the two men.

"What's with Mutt and Jeff?" she asked.

"I don't know, I mean they're dressed like businessmen, but their hands are rough, as if they are laborers. They're polite and quiet enough, but they aren't really eating lunch. Kind of creepy, the way they keep looking at the art gallery and not saying anything," the first waitress replied.

"Well, you better take 'em their check or the boss will get on you for not doing your job."

The first waitress walked over to the table and gave the men their check.

"Can I get you gents anything else?" she asked.

As she set the check down, they suddenly got to their feet. Their quickness startled the waitress, even though, their manner towards her was apologetic. The heftier of the two, Mr. Jones, reached into his pocket and pulled out a twenty and put it into the waitress's palm.

"Keep the change," he said.

The waitress looked down at her hand and started to protest that it was way too much, but the duo were already out of the cafe and headed across the street to the art gallery.

She looked at the check for three-fifty and at the twenty and smiled. They were definitely odd, but the tip made up for that. Too bad more customers didn't tip like them. She started cleaning off the table and looked out the window and noticed the pair enter the art gallery. How strange, she thought, they didn't look like the type to be interested in art.

The manager of the Vieux Carre Gallery quickly responded to the bell as a stylish young woman dressed in a shape fitting suit entered carrying a large portfolio case. The young woman would easily turn heads anywhere she went, but Charles Devue was more interested in her case than the young woman herself.

"Mademoiselle Reneau," he said, "what a pleasure it is to see you again."

Devue was unaware he was standing in front a revealing nude study of the young woman hanging on the wall behind him. Mademoiselle Reneau looked up at the painting and then back at Mr. Devue and smiled shyly, not from innocence, but more from an inside joke. Devue noticed her shift in gaze and turned his head to see what she had glanced at. He became flustered and apologetic and she enjoyed his embarrassment but not to the point of rudeness. She calmed his apprehension and assured him she was not offended, which she wasn't.

Devue quickly changed the subject, he was anxious to see what the young woman had in the portfolio. Martin Stanton paintings were selling extremely well. He was an infamous celebrity because of the unsubstantiated relationship between his family and the New York mob. That he died mysteriously, made his artwork highly collectible. Since he wouldn't be painting any more, the limited number of paintings available and the scandalous circumstances surrounding his death artificially increased the paintings' value.

Devue shook with anticipation much like a high strung small dog as Mademoiselle Reneau opened the portfolio.

"Of course, Mademoiselle Reneau, you have the appropriate provenance and the necessary documentation to prove you are the legitimate owner of the paintings," he said.

"As you know, Monsieur Devue," said the young woman,"I was Martin's model for a number of months."

She paused at the catch in her breath presenting a moment of grief.

"It has been in all the papers. And Martin was a fastidious personality who kept very accurate records about his work. I have letters from him describing our relationship, well in very intimate details as well as documents assigning the paintings to me. Is that what you are looking for?" she asked lowering her eyes.

"Oh, my dear, I do not mean to pry, but with the recent news stories about poor Martin, we in the industry must be most careful, you understand. I am sure your provenance is in order and as soon as I can confirm that, I will be most happy to help in the disposition of your beloved possessions."

Mademoiselle Reneau cared little for Devue's false sincerity, she was more interested in the amount of money he was going to hand her. She continued the act of grieving model as she placed the portfolio upon the counter for the gallery manager to peruse. She had a brief image of the charwoman, laundress, and undertaker putting forth their ill-gotten booty before old Joe from "A Christmas Carol" to collect what was rightfully due them.

Devue began taking out the paintings, and as if on cue, the bell to the gallery sounded announcing the door was opening again. Two men is suits entered the gallery. Mr. Devue smiled as they entered. Mademoiselle Reneau looked up and maintained character, while she didn't know the two gentlemen, she had seen them in the cafe across the street. It was clear that Devue was expecting them. That meant they were there to confirm the authenticity of Martin's paintings. If they truly were valid authoritative experts, she knew she had no reason to be concerned. These really were paintings that had been identified as painted by Martin Stanton.

"Mademoiselle Reneau, these are the two gentlemen here to authenticate the paintings. They are Misters Brown and Jones. Gentlemen this is Mademoiselle Reneau, Martin Stanton's model for a number of his paintings," said Devue gesturing at the one on the wall.

Mr. Brown and Mr. Jones looked up at the nude painting of Mademoiselle Reneau hanging on the wall and for a few moments admired the artistry of the piece, though they did linger to admire the model herself. Each cleared his throat and offered his condolences on Martin's passing. Mademoiselle Reneau offered her hand for an appropriate greeting and both men flubbed the process of taking it properly. Mademoiselle Reneau was careful not to be offended by their clumsiness. At least they didn't slobber. After all, these gentlemen were about to make her a very rich woman.

Devue carefully placed the six unframed paintings on easels standing in a row against the gallery wall. Mr. Jones and Mr. Brown carefully examined them. Mr. Brown consulted a notebook as he examined them. Mr. Jones just looked and nodded as Mr. Brown confirmed the legitimacy of each painting.

"At auction, these could bring well over three

hundred grand, er thousand dollars," said Mr. Brown. "Mademoiselle Reneau, you do have papers proving uh authenticated ownership?"

Mademoiselle Reneau went to the case and produced several letters that had been appropriately witnessed that the paintings were hers. Mr. Brown examined the letters with the same attention to detail he had examined the paintings. He handed the documentation back to her and nodded to Devue.

"Everything seems to be in order, Mr. Devue, these are authentic Martin Stanton paintings, and clearly Mademoiselle Reneau owns them," he said.

Devue clasped his hands and rubbed them together.

"I'm not looking to auction them, Monsieur Devue, I am looking to sell them," said the young woman.

"Of course my dear, " said Devue. "Gentlemen, I thank you for your time, and of course the gallery will pass on your compensation to your employer. Mademoiselle Reneau and I have private business to conduct, so if you don't mind..."

Mr. Brown and Mr. Jones had concluded part of their assignment. The paintings were legitimate, as was Mademoiselle Reneau. Their only task left was to determine if Martin Stanton was dead. They were quick to say their good-byes and offer their condolences once again to Mademoiselle

Reneau. Each again flubbed the gesture with her offered hand, more because they were sideways gazing at the nude hanging on the wall then from clumsiness. Again they cleared their throats and headed out of the shop. They crossed the street and paused to see if they were being watched.

Devue and the young woman were occupied in an animated discussion and the two men quickly got into a car and waited.

"Mademoiselle Reneau, I am authorized to offer you twenty-five thousand dollars per painting," said Devue.

"And yet you will give me forty," she said.

"Mademoiselle Reneau...," said Devue.

"There are other galleries, Monsieur Devue," she said, "And I have more paintings."

"More, mmm, ...more," he stammered.

"More," she said.

"I have to make a phone call," said Devue.

"Please do, I am in no hurry," she said.

As Mademoiselle Reneau left the gallery, she noticed the two men in the car. She smiled, she had expected they had ulterior motives other than to just authenticate Martin's paintings. She held the case close to her body and hurried to the bank. She had not realized how much two hundred forty thousand dollars weighed. She was astonished that Devue had that much cash available for her to take.

She entered the bank and went to a desk

asking to have access to a safe deposit box for which she had a key. The bank attendant confirmed her signature and led her to the vault with the boxes. Two keys were used to open the box lock and Mademoiselle Reneau was escorted to a room where she could open the box in privacy.

After the attendant left she opened the box and looked at the money already inside. She was tempted by the additional cash, but her partner knew how much was in the box so she ignored the impulse. She put two hundred thousand dollars into the safety deposit box and closed it up. Then she proceeded to conceal forty thousand dollars on her person. She exited the room and returned with the attendant to replace the safe deposit box in the vault.

She left the bank. She had lightened herself of the portfolio case and could now move more swiftly while walking along the sidewalk. When she was in France after the war, she often had to lose unwanted pursuers quickly and she had become quite adept at it. She immediately spotted the car after leaving the bank. She didn't know what Mr. Jones or Mr. Brown did for a living, but unobtrusive surveillance was not it. She decided on a non-nonchalant form of losing her newly acquired admirers rather than ducking in and out through the various obstacles available to her. She didn't want to alert her pursuers that they had been made.

She walked along the avenue as if window shopping. She stopped at a dress shop and acted as if she was excited about a dress in the window. She entered the shop and made a show of talking to a sale's girl in full view from outside the shop. The car parked in view of the shop window, and her two spectators hunkered down in their car seats and waited for her to exit the shop.

The Young woman explained to the sales girl, she was being followed. She asked if there was an exit in the rear of the shop. Upon confirmation, she offered to buy the dress in the window and provided a generous tip if the sales girl would pretend to service her in the dressing room after she left out the back.

The door to the dressing room was also visible from the front window. So for fifteen minutes the shop girl took various dresses to the door of the dressing room, and proceeded to hang them up inside. She would periodically return and take dresses away. After about fifteen minutes, she ended the charade and went about her normal business.

It took Mr. Jones and Mr. Brown another five minutes to realized there was no longer any activity at the dressing room. Mr. Jones exited the car and entered the shop, he spoke to the shop girl who was quite skilled at acting scattered and finally in frustration, Mr. Jones headed for the door. The shop girl patted her pocket and smiled as he left.

Mr. Brown sat behind the wheel as he waited for Mr. Jones to return to the car. Mr. Brown could tell by his partner's manner as he returned to the car, that the girl had eluded them. The gallery had been their only link to the girl. From an earlier conversation with Mr. Devue, they had determined he had no idea where the girl was staying. They had been told to keep a low profile, and now they had to report back to Mr. Smith. Mr. Jones sat down in the car and closed the door.

"Let's go back to the hotel," he said. "We'll call Mr. Smith from there."

"The girl was to provide us with proof as to whether Stanton was alive or not," said Mr. Brown.

"What do we tell Mr. Smith?" asked Mr. Jones.

"The Truth."

Mademoiselle Reneau was wearing a dress from the shop appearing very different. She continued looking around her as she made her way to the apartment. She found it comforting that the streets of New Orleans reminded her of the streets of Orleans in France. She felt at home as she backtracked and checked landmarks and the people, who were going about their normal business. Her two shadows would have been noticeable in a moments glance. She did see the car after she had left the dress shop, but she was quick to confirm that they were headed away from her and had no idea where she was.

Remaining vigilant, the young woman made one additional stop at a different small bank before returning home. Here she deposited forty thousand dollars in her own personal safe deposit box. She breathed a sigh of relief as she exited the bank. Walking in a lighter step she entered her apartment building and took the elevator to the third floor. She took out her keys, opened the door, and entered the apartment.

"Mon Cheri, I am back," she called.

"How did it go?" asked Martin.

"Mr. Devue was most generous, he paid two hundred thousand for the six paintings," she said.

"Didn't I tell you this was going to be easy," he said

Mademoiselle Reneau slipped her arms around Martin's neck and kissed him passionately. Slowly he broke away from her.

"The key, Michelle, give me the key to the safe deposit box, please," he said.

The young woman pouted her lips, she looked down, and surrendered the key to Martin.

"But when can we go to France. You promised," she said.

"Six more paintings," he said.

Martin had walked away from Michelle.

"But Mr. Devue was most generous, I told him I had more."

He stopped and turned on her.

"You shouldn't have done that," he said. "Too

many paintings in one location can have an adverse effect on the price. Remember I am supposed to be dead. We don't want too much exposure in a single location. No, the next gallery needs to be out of the French Quarter."

Martin walked back to a pouting Michelle and took her in his arms and kissed her.

"I promise you Cheri, when we get half a million, it's hello, France, here we come."

He kissed her again and slapped her on the ass. He walked over to a table where he was sitting and reading the paper. He sat down and picked up a cup of coffee. Michelle walked up behind him and massaged his shoulders.

"You were right about the men being there to authenticate the paintings," she said.

"A Mr. Brown and Jones," he said.

"Qui. They waited for me outside," she said.

"Really," he said, "and what happened?"

"They were amateurs," she said. "I spotted them easily. I let them follow me for a bit and then I lost them at a dress shop. That is where I bought this little number, it is correct, little number?"

Martin pulled her onto his lap and kissed her slowly as he let his hands wander about her hips.

"You are such a good little spy," he said.

Michelle sighed and smiled, she raised her eyes and let her mind wander. Martin watched her and finally interrupted her thoughts.

"What? Is there anything else?" he asked.

"I was just thinking, there was one man, back in France, I could have never lost him. It is a good thing he is a drunk in San Francisco and not here in New Orleans. From him we might find trouble."

"Even as a drunk?" asked Martin.

"He was a man never to underestimate, Mon Cheri. But enough, what do you read?" she asked.

"Actually I was reading about some private detective in San Francisco that got himself killed. He was working for my widow. Small world, huh?

"Anyway he had a new partner. The police and this new guy took care of the men who killed the detective. Seems they were some ex-partners of mine. Here take a look."

Martin handed Michelle the paper and she started reading the story. Suddenly her eyes got very big and she looked a little frightened.

"Cheri, what's wrong?" he asked.

"Jonas Watcher, he was the man in France. He can be very dangerous," she said.

Mr. Brown picked up the phone and dialed. Mr. Jones sat nervously opposite him and waited.

"Mr. Smith?" asked Mr. Brown.

"Yes," said the voice on the other end of the phone.

"This is Mr. Brown," he said.

"Continue, " said Mr. Smith.

"We made contact with the model at the Vieux Carre Gallery. It was definitely her, there was a painting of her hanging on the wall. Anyway, I inspected the artwork, and it had all the hallmarks that you said should be present. She also had documents proving that she owned them. The gallery owner called it provo something," Mr. Brown said.

"Provenance," sighed Mr. Smith, "and what else?"

"We followed her for a short time, but we lost her while she was shopping," said Mr. Brown.

"Were you spotted?" asked Mr. Smith.

"I don't think so," Mr. Brown replied.

"I see. Thank you, gentlemen. Return to New York, your assignment in New Orleans is over. I am sure your employer has other work for you."

The phone went dead and Mr. Jones stared at Mr. Brown.

"Well?" Mr. Jones asked.

"We are to return to New York," said Mr. Brown, "He was disappointed, but I think we're okay."

In New York:

In the darkened office, two men sat opposite each other at a desk. Mr. Smith sat behind the desk in an office chair. His employer sat in a plush client chair. Both men were smoking cigars and drinking single malt. Mr. Smith hung up the phone, slumped in his chair and sighed.

"Your employees leave much to be desired," he said. "The girl clearly spotted them, and they have no clue."

"I am not sending my best to New Orleans on this," his employer said. "The bank is whole again. With the money from the bank books that you brought back, we have been more than compensated. Besides it was Stanton's son, and he doesn't care what we do to him. By your own testimony, he wasn't the instigator. I'm thinking of hiring it out, cheap."

"Then it will come back to you," said Mr. Smith.

"What do you recommend?" asked the employer.

"Let me handle it."

"What will you do?"

"I will have Jonas Watcher and Lieutenant Sanders find out if he is really alive," said Mr. Smith.

"Why would they?"

"Justice, Martin Stanton is not a nice man."

Mr. Smith's employer rolled his eyes.

"You've read the report on Watcher," said Mr. Smith. "If he thinks Stanton might be alive, he'll find him. We'll have Stanton Senior contact Watcher, and ask him to find out what really happened to his son."

"And why would Sanders get involved?" asked the employer.

"You have friends in New Orleans government, pull some strings," suggested Mr. Smith.

"Wouldn't it be easier just to buy the cop?"

"Not for sale," said Mr. Smith.

"Then threaten his wife."

"No!" said Mr. Smith.

The sharp retort caused Mr. Smith's employer to sit back in his chair.

"Is there something there?" he asked.

"Respect," said Mr. Smith. "She had a thirty-eight out threatening my manhood before I could react. If you want Martin Stanton found, then you'll do it my way, otherwise write it off."

"You know I can't. I would be overrun by every punk in New York if I did."

Mr. Smiths employer shook his head and then nodded.

"You handle it," he said.

"No, Jonas Watcher will handle it."

Back in San Francisco:

I was staring out the window of my office as the evening fog started to roll in. Drifts of mist crept just above the street below slowly hiding people as they walked into the distance. The light from the street lamps began to glow as they caught water droplets. Jeez, I was getting romantic.

Betty had gone for the day. We had just

wrapped up a child abduction, successfully bringing parents and child back together. I was feeling pretty good about this job.

The phone rang, and I was hesitant to answer it, but my better nature kicked in.

"Hello, Jonas Watcher, Investigations," I said.

"Mr. Watcher, this is Martin Stanton Senior, could we talk?"

I swear there were woman laughing in the background somewhere. The Sisters Fate were not done with me yet.

Thank You

Thank you for reading my book. If you enjoyed it, won't you please take a moment to leave me a review at your favorite retailer?

Thank you again.

Gene Poschman

Look for my next book

Jonas Watcher:

The Case of the Bourbon Street Hustler

About the Author:

Gene Poschman

I am a native Californian, I married my High School Sweetheart. We are coming up on being married for 50 years, why she puts up with me is beyond me. I have been a frustrated writer for most of my working career having to settle for writing white papers and technical training manuals. I have always been an avid watcher of film noir, mysteries and other detective crime fiction as well as science fiction and fantasy.

I read quite a bit which would probably surprise a number of my teachers. I would have been a better reader earlier if Dick and Jane were detectives, or at least a wizard and witch. I grew up on a farm, boring.

I have written numerous unpublished short stories and two novels, which shared the same fate, probably for good reason.

The rest is subject to change on my personal whim.

Made in the USA
San Bernardino, CA
19 May 2015